From New York Times and USA Today bestselling author Thea Harrison comes the final novella featuring Pia and Dragos…

Pia's latest pregnancy has become a daily challenge, her relationship with Dragos strained with argument. That hasn't stopped them from achieving a compromise and traveling to Las Vegas to celebrate their friend Rune's wedding to his mate Carling.

From the moment they arrive, the trip goes awry. Death walks in Vegas, and Pia is kidnapped as an ancient enemy makes a move to destroy the Great Beast once and for all.

But the Great Beast has other plans.

On Planet Dragos everything goes the way he arranges it—unless someone decides to cross him, and God help them then, because he doesn't know how to back down, and he doesn't ever, ever let up….

Planet Dragos

Thea Harrison

Prologue

Devil's Gate, Nevada

DISASTERS WERE ALWAYS a surprise, Dragos thought.

He raced through the bizarre forest, his heart pounding a thunderous rhythm in his ears. Branches of alien-looking foliage and creeping vines whipped his face and arms as he exploded through the tangled underbrush like a heat-seeking missile.

Dragos had a wide-ranging vision, and he knew how to play a very long game. If he saw something coming, even if it took decades for the event to occur, he maneuvered to either avoid or confront it. Sometimes he chose to go to war, but when he did, he always calculated the cost.

Often in recent centuries, he employed his relatively new-fangled skill for politicking, and the dragon smiled cynically to himself as he treated with the smaller, weaker creatures around him.

They were all so eager to believe they were important, so credulous that he saw them as important too, and so remarkably easy to manipulate. Whereas, really, the most dangerous and important things about them were their strength in mass numbers and their ability to propagate at an alarming rate.

He didn't call any of those things *disasters*. Those were situations that he handled, and he handled them well.

No, disasters were something else entirely. Disasters were the small child suddenly gone missing or the explosion in the face that took away vitally important chunks of memory.

Or his mate in danger.

That one. *Disaster* was too puny a word for that one. That was an apocalypse waiting to happen, because if the dragon lost his mate, he would not crumble meekly in some humble demise. No, he would set the whole world on fire and drag it down with him into the dark and never care that it would destroy the other people he might have once loved.

Dragos castigated himself viciously. This was his fault. He should have known how bad the trouble would be from the moment it had appeared on their horizon. The warning signs had been there, but he had been too preoccupied to take proper note.

As soon as he had discovered that Death had come to Las Vegas, he should have grabbed Pia, turned on his heel, and gone home.

Death only appeared in person for the extraordinary events.

Chapter One

"I CAN GET myself out," Pia said irritably when Dragos stuck his hand inside the limo.

He bent to look in at her, one black eyebrow raised. The Bellagio Hotel and Casino was busy, and they had parked to one side of the main entrance, half the limousine out of the shade of the gigantic, ornate portico.

Slanting, laser-like sunshine lined the edge of Dragos's tough, bronzed features and black hair in radiant white. The desert sun was nothing like the sun in upstate New York. It was harsh and unforgiving here and, despite the luxurious, glittering city that sprawled around them, potentially lethal.

Dragos did not appear to be discomfited by the difference in climate, and he never needed to wear sunglasses to protect his eyes—he only wore sunglasses to maintain a barrier between him and the outside world.

He was the only physical creature Pia knew who could look directly at the sun and not be blinded by it.

Whenever sunlight bathed him, he grew more burnished and vital, as if the fire that lived inside the dragon recognized the fire from the sun and gained nourishment from it.

His gold gaze narrowed. "You've always accepted my help before."

She could tell his feelings weren't hurt. He had the strongest psyche of anyone Pia had ever met. She could probably drive over and reverse on his feelings repeatedly with an eighty-thousand-pound eighteen-wheeler before she managed to put a dent in them.

No, he was simply, genuinely baffled.

Realizing she was being irrational, she breathed deeply for a moment before she explained, "I accepted your help before because it was sexy."

And right now nothing was sexy. Not even him.

He gave her rounded belly a significant glance. "But you're so big you actually need my help this time."

"I'm so big," she repeated in a flat voice. If there had been a table anywhere in reach, she would have been sorely tempted to flip it. "Thank you so much for pointing that out to me, Dragos. I hadn't noticed how big I am. If it weren't for you, that fact would have flown right by me. Now, if you'll just move out of my way, I'll get my own big damn self out of this car."

He angled his jaw and his expression turned calculating, but he straightened and stepped back without saying another word.

Then Pia had to rock a few times before she got

enough momentum to hoist herself up so she could lumber out. Moisture from the Bellagio's famous fountains wafted against her cheeks, blown by the hot desert wind.

Gah. That must have looked horrible. She was so ungainly. She had *never* been ungainly before, not even when she had been at her biggest with her first pregnancy. Then, she had felt sleek and powerful, like she'd been a sex goddess and a mother goddess all rolled into one.

The times she and Dragos had shared during her first pregnancy... Then, everything had been sexy. Newly mated, they had burned up the bedsheets with an insatiable need for each other.

As Dragos opened his mouth, she angled her head away and held up a forefinger as she muttered, "Don't say a word. I got the job done. That's all that matters."

Standing a few steps behind Dragos, Eva held Pia's Kate Spade purse and waited, lips pressed together and dark eyes snapping. Her face was certainly expressive of something, but after studying Eva's bold features, Pia decided she didn't need to know.

Pia took her purse and told the other woman telepathically, *I don't want to hear a word from you either.*

Me? Eva's eyebrows shot up. *I would never!*

Eva's mental tone was so pious, her lie so enormous, Pia had to laugh in spite of herself.

She turned to Dragos. "I'm sorry I'm so crabby."

His eyes gleamed in a subtle smile. "You're very

pregnant," he told her. "And as you are well aware, I've read several books about pregnancy. I've decided to consider you somewhat insane until the baby is born."

They had flown to Las Vegas to attend Rune and Carling's wedding, and for the trip he had dressed in jeans and a black T-shirt that hugged the muscles in his chest and arms. From his military-short black hair to his scuffed boots, he was at his plainest and most unvarnished.

But that didn't mean he could go unnoticed. At six-foot-eight, Dragos towered over everyone else around him. His Power was so intense it shimmered around him in an invisible corona like heat rising off the pavement. She had seen the same effect in others from the first generation of the Elder Races, those who had sprung into existence when the Earth was formed.

But for some reason, Dragos's Power felt hotter and fiercer than even the oldest of the old that Pia had met. She suspected that too was because of his Wyr form. The dragon was a creature of fire, and everyone around him seemed paler and smaller by comparison.

Behind him, a multitude of people hurried to do their jobs. The Cadillac SUV transporting Dr. Medina and Aryal, one of the Wyr sentinels, had pulled up behind the limo, and they had climbed out. Aryal impatiently directed guards and bellhops who piled luggage onto wheeled racks.

While Dragos stood ignoring them all, his attention solely focused on her, they orbited around him like satellites as they did his bidding.

She'd been lying to herself. His brutal handsomeness and raw masculinity tugged at her even when she was at her most tired and cranky. He was always the sexiest thing she had ever seen, and it was never subtle.

No, she was the one who wasn't sexy anymore. She felt huge, puffy, and clumsy, like the Stay Puft Marshmallow Man that had rampaged New York in *Ghostbusters*, and the only way she could hide the dark circles that seemed to have taken up permanent residence underneath her eyes was with a liberal application of concealer.

She caught sight of a tall, leggy blonde walking past them. The woman had supermodel good looks and wore a halter top and shorts so short they showed a hint of lacy purple underwear. Completing the outfit were cowboy boots, long dangly earrings, and a cowboy hat. She stared at Dragos with such single-minded hunger she walked into a nearby bush, apologized to it absently, and moved on.

Meanwhile, Aryal strode over to Dragos and they talked together in low voices. Dragos had never even noticed the leggy blonde woman or her antics.

Pia didn't know whether she wanted to snarl or laugh. Maybe both?

She rubbed her face instead and struggled to get a grip on her unruly emotions. Dragos was indisputably hers. They were married, and in the unique way that Wyr had, they had bonded for life.

Still, the part of her that had gone somewhat insane whispered that their mating bond only ensured they would be mated for the rest of their lives. It didn't guarantee anything about sexual fidelity or enduring love.

Meanwhile, the drug protocol she needed to take daily in order to bring their unborn son safely to term had dampened her immune system. When she had been pregnant with her first son, the only weight she had gained was baby weight. Even when she had been eight months pregnant, she could have run for miles, a particular talent she took from her Wyr form.

This time she had already gained far too much weight, and Stinkpot wasn't born yet. Just the thought of running made her want to lie down and take a nap, and a perpetual low-level anxiety chewed at her like mice nibbling at the electrical conduits in a house. She felt frayed and frumpy. She'd had no idea how much her self-esteem had been tied to her looks until she'd lost them.

Besides, Eva said, amusement lacing her voice, *even if I did want to say something, I'm on your side.*

Pia started and glanced at the other woman. She had been so preoccupied with her own miserable thoughts she'd forgotten that she and Eva had been talking telepathically. Her memory and attention span were other casualties of this pregnancy.

Oh yeah?

Eva shrugged. *He might have read several pregnancy books, but that don't make him no expert on nothing. Nobody should tell their baby mama she too big to get herself out of a car. Men really are from Mars, I guess.*

Men might be from Mars, Pia said, *and women could possibly be from Venus, but Dragos is a planet all on his own. Just look how everyone revolves around him. On Planet Dragos everything goes the way he arranges it—unless you decide to cross him, and God help you then, because he doesn't know how to back down, and he doesn't ever, ever let up.*

She had been reaching for lighthearted and amused, but that comment had come out sharper than she had meant it to.

Eva asked, *You guys still fighting?*

Yep. She could feel Eva studying her profile but refused to look in the other woman's direction. *I don't want to talk about it.*

After a small silence, Eva said finally, *Well, if you ever do, let me know. I'm here for you.*

Thanks. Pia tried to smile, but she had a feeling it came out all twisted.

Dragos touched her arm. "I've got to talk to Aryal, but there's no reason for you to wait while I do. Why don't you go inside where it's cooler?"

"Sounds good."

As she and Eva turned to the front doors of their hotel, Pia glanced in the direction where the supermodel blonde had been walking, but the other woman had disappeared.

A flash of light caught her attention. She looked up to see Dragos's figure featured on a billboard surrounded with colored lights.

Wait, what?

Jolted out of her preoccupation, she stared more closely as a shadow passed over the sun. The scene on the billboard was a luxurious nightclub filled with dark shadows, white and gold lights, and red roses.

A powerful figure of a man stood on a stage. He wore a black suit and was in silhouette, half turned away. Twisting at the waist to look back over one wide shoulder at the camera, he held out a hand as if beckoning the onlooker. One corner of the billboard read LAST DANCE, THE MIDNIGHT LOUNGE, RIVERVIEW HOTEL & CASINO.

It wasn't Dragos. It couldn't be. The man had the same black hair, but upon closer examination, he appeared to be slimmer. The only thing she could tell for sure about his lean face was that he appeared to have green eyes.

"How odd," she murmured. "Dragos, do you know who that is? He looks like you."

Like Pia, he had been in midmotion as he turned back to Aryal, who was arguing with someone over the phone. He paused to look in the same direction as she did, and his expression hardened.

"He's nobody," Dragos said. "Ignore him."

Aryal walked up, held her phone out to Dragos, and snapped, "You talk to him. I'm done."

Dragos gave the billboard one last, long look. Then he bent his head to kiss Pia's cheek. He told her, "This may take a little while."

"No problem," Pia said as she tilted her head up to him. He hadn't exactly answered her question, had he?

The sensation of his warm lips lingered on her skin as he held the phone up to his ear and strode back to Aryal. The shadow across the sun darkened further.

Dragos walked by behind her. He said in her ear, "Why don't you come see me?"

Wait, no. That wasn't Dragos's voice.

Dragos was not behind her either. She had watched him walk away as he talked to whoever had put Aryal into a temper.

Frowning, Pia spun in a slow circle, looking for the tall, dark man who had spoken into her ear.

There wasn't anybody nearby. Eva had not yet noticed that Pia had stopped to have an exchange with Dragos and had continued walking to the hotel's front doors where Dr. Medina had joined her. Pia stood alone among the swirl and eddy of people.

The day brightened again. As she glanced up, the sky was a clear, cloudless blue.

Maybe the desert heat was getting to her. Maybe she had hallucinated the whole thing.

Did she believe that?

She shook her head. Nope. She did not.

Lips pursed, she strode over to Dr. Medina and Eva. "We don't have anything on the schedule until the wedding reception this evening. Carling's probably sleeping, and in any case it's not polite to bother a

Vampyre in the middle of the day unless there's an emergency. I'm sure Rune is around somewhere, but he'll be busy doing whatever it is guys do in Las Vegas the day before their wedding. Anybody up for a little sightseeing this afternoon?"

"You know I'll go," Eva said.

"Yeah, well, you kind of have to." Pia gave the other woman an affectionate push with one shoulder. "Seeing as you're my bodyguard and all."

With a grin, Eva nudged her back. When they'd met, they had been at odds with each other, but despite the rocky beginning they had become fast friends.

Dr. Medina watched them, smiling. "I'll pass. After I check your vitals, I've got some patients I need to call."

Pia's smile faded, but daily checkups with Dr. Medina, along with the doctor's attendance on this trip, was the compromise she had suggested to Dragos after they'd had their worst argument to date.

So she said, "You bet. Let's get it done."

Two of their guards had already completed the check-in procedure and had gone to clear the suite, and Pia, Dr. Medina, and Eva headed for the Spa Tower. The Bellagio resort was huge, so it was a bit of a hike.

Once they reached the luxurious penthouse suite, Dr. Medina checked Pia's blood pressure and heart rate, scanned the baby magically, then gave Pia her daily shot of the drug protocol.

"All good?" Pia asked when the doctor was finished.

The older woman gave her a smile. "Everything is fine. Have fun sightseeing."

"Thanks."

Even though she had been given the all clear, she hesitated, torn.

Other people were arriving for the wedding, and Carling and Rune had reserved an entire floor in the Spa Tower for the wedding guests.

Of Dragos's original sentinels, Aryal had flown in with Dragos and Pia, and Bayne, Graydon, and his mate, Beluviel, would be arriving later in the afternoon. The two newer sentinels, Alexander and Aryal's mate, Quentin, had remained back in New York, while Tiago and his mate, Niniane, were in Adriyel and unable to attend.

Rune and Carling also had friends from Florida who would either already be here or arriving soon—Duncan and Seremela, Grace and Khalil, and Claudia and Luis—but Pia didn't know any of those couples very well.

Part of her felt as if she should stay and be social, but the other part...

The other part didn't want to look into their faces as they saw how much she had changed.

She would have to face the others soon enough this evening. For now she was going to give herself permission to avoid everything.

She jotted a quick note for Dragos on hotel stationery and left it in a prominent place on the hall table by the suite's double doors. Then, grabbing her purse, she said to Eva, "Let's get out of here."

"Where are we going?"

"To the Riverview Casino."

Chapter Two

FIFTEEN MINUTES LATER, Pia and Eva walked into the Riverview. Like the other Las Vegas great hotels and casinos, the Riverview glittered with flashing lights and luxurious appointments—marble floors, soaring ceilings, and lavish works of art.

Unlike the other hotels and casinos, the Riverview was under the sole ownership of an Elder Races company, the Light Fae Queen Tatiana's Northern Lights.

While a proportion of Elder Races creatures were scattered throughout the rest of the city, here they were in the majority. Demonkind servers walked by, carrying trays of drinks. Nearby, a medusa sat playing slots at three adjacent machines, his head snakes wrapped firmly around the handles. Pia stared at him, fascinated.

"Ah, Las Vegas," Eva said as they walked across the open floor. "The Cirque du Soleil, Cher, Ricky Martin, Paul Simon… So many great things to do, so little time. Did you know that Vampyres love the fake sky at the Venetian Resort? They have gondola rides down the Grand Canal, and it's all inside. Want to get in a little slot machine action?"

"What?" Glancing at the other woman, Pia realized Eva had noticed the direction she was staring. She was probably being rude by staring so openly, not that the medusa would notice. His concentration on the slot machines was total. "I'm not a gambler."

"Oh, come on. Live a little," Eva coaxed. "I could get you some chips, and we could try our luck at one of the tables."

Pia laughed. "I still remember how hard I worked to make money. I'm not comfortable throwing it away at blackjack or roulette."

"I bet Dragos wouldn't be throwing his money away." Eva grinned. "I'd love to see that dragon in a poker game."

"That's not going to happen here," Pia told her. "Dragos is banned from gambling in Las Vegas. He's too good at counting cards, and nobody with any sense will sit in on a poker game with him. All he can do is see some shows and attend Rune and Carling's wedding."

Eva laughed. "You didn't tell me why you wanted to come to the Riverview instead of hanging out at the Bellagio."

"I'm looking for the Midnight Lounge. There's a show called *Last Dance* that I want to check into." Scanning the area, she caught sight of a sign. "It's over there, down that hall."

Eva kept pace beside her. Stepping inside the Midnight Lounge was somewhat disappointing. While it was indisputably the scene from the billboard, the photoshopped magic was missing. Except for a ghoul mopping the floor and another one working behind the bar, the lounge was empty and the stage dark.

"Vegas may never sleep, but they've got to mop the floors some time." Eva regarded both ghouls with a smile.

Pia frowned. The damn drug protocol not only damped her immune system, it also muffled her ability to sense magic. She asked, "Can you sense anything? Any residual Power or magic?"

"Nothing out of the ordinary. Sparks here and there, magic items, individual people. It comes and goes. There are dampening fields all over casinos so players can't communicate with each other telepathically or cheat with other kinds of spells." Eva looked at her thoughtfully. "Why? What are you looking for?"

"Anything. Nothing." She shrugged. "I had a weird moment back at the Bellagio. And there was somebody that looked like Dragos on the billboard for this show, but obviously it wasn't him. When I asked Dragos about it, he brushed me off and told me to ignore it."

Eva raised an eyebrow. "So naturally you thought to run right over here."

When Eva put it like that, Pia felt a little sheepish. "I was running away from the hotel as much as anything."

"You said you had a weird moment." Eva frowned, hands on her hips as she surveyed the area. "I'm not a fan of weird, but I don't see or sense any danger."

"Weird isn't necessarily bad. Just look at our lives. Every single thing in it could be labeled *weird*." Pia headed to the bar where an older ghoul unloaded a dishwasher and stacked the clean glasses on a shelf. "Excuse me—is *Last Dance* showing here?"

He shrugged. Like all ghouls, he had a long, mournful face. "Sure. Maybe. I don't actually know. This is my first day back at work after a two-week vacation. After a while all the shows start to look alike, know what I mean?"

"I guess so." Amused, she glanced at Eva, who had approached the other ghoul.

"Hey, buddy," Eva said. "Anybody back in the dressing rooms?"

He paused to lean on the handle of his mop as if he were too tired to stand upright. "Might be."

Eva handed him a few twenties. "Why don't you check for us? If there is someone back there, could you tell them we'd like to speak to them?"

"Okay." Pocketing the cash, he shuffled toward the back.

As they waited, Pia strolled over to look at the stage. It was decorated the same as the scene in the billboard, with tall ebony vases filled with long-stemmed red roses. Impulsively, she walked up the three steps to stand on the stage. There was a trapdoor in the middle of the worn floor.

As she viewed the lounge from her new vantage place, the stage lights switched on. White light hit her full in the face, blinding her, while the rest of the lounge receded into darkness.

"Sorry, did I trigger that?" she called out as she threw up a hand to shield her eyes.

From behind the shelter of her fingers, she could make out Eva's outline where she waited by a table. The muted figure of a ghoul walked up to her, and they talked. They both seemed very far away, and neither one of them appeared to notice Pia.

"Eva?" she said uncertainly. If there was one thing Eva should be doing, it was noticing Pia, especially when she called out to her. "Eva!"

The other woman gave no indication she'd heard. And that wasn't the good kind of weird.

Booted heels sounded on the hardwood floor, and a tall man came to stand beside her. As Pia looked at him, her heart began to race.

He had a hard profile, much like Dragos's, and he had the same black hair, broad shoulders, and strong, sensual mouth.

"Hello, Pia Giovanni Cuelebre," he said. His voice was deep and not quite unfamiliar.

Her leg muscles clenched until she stood on the balls of her feet, ready to run. She sensed nothing from him— no danger, no magic. No Power. But Eva wasn't answering her, and this man knew her full name.

Taking a wary step back, she asked, "Do I know you?"

"I know you. We came close to meeting once."

Turning toward her, the man smiled. His eyes were green. "You were pregnant with your first son then. He saved your life, almost at the expense of his."

That kicked her pulse into higher gear. Nobody except Dragos knew what her peanut had done, back when she had suffered a wound that had nearly turned mortal. She whispered, "How do you know that?"

He was much more handsome than Dragos if the truth were told. Magnetically so. But he carried the same kind of blade in his smile. "The same way I know how much your mother loves you. She told you that you could go to her if you wished. Remember?"

Shock moved through her like a slow-shifting glacier, numbing her hands and lips. "I never told anybody about that, not even Dragos. *Who are you?*"

"You can call me Rael if you like." Putting his hands in his pockets, he shifted to look out over the near-empty lounge.

A thought occurred to her, as preposterous and vast as an ocean. It couldn't be, but… so many things in her life were preposterous. Were *weird*.

"Rael, as in…" Her voice shook, and she had to swallow and start again. "As in Azrael?"

He neither confirmed nor denied it. Like a mountain, he simply was. "You know, everybody was so surprised by you when Dragos took a mate. It was the last thing anybody expected. You've taught him how to love something more than himself, but long ago and for many centuries he was known as the Great Beast. The Great

Beast made powerful, long-lived mortal enemies, and they remember. Never forget, Pia Giovanni Cuelebre— you and your children are his greatest triumph, but you are also his biggest weakness."

Yeah, yeah, she'd heard that before. She fast-forwarded through it impatiently to focus on the most important thing.

"My mom," Pia breathed. "Can—Would you let me talk to her? Please?"

He shook his head. "She is not here, Pia."

"But she was, back then."

"Back then you were close enough to dying you could hear her."

"Is that what I need to do in order to hear her again?"

Turning his head, Death speared her with one of those bladelike smiles. "Do you want to get close enough to death again to find out?"

"I guess not," she whispered.

Her thinking crumbled into shambles. Unless she was hallucinating, she was actually in conversation with one of the world's Primal Powers. Questions and fears piled up on each other.

"Why—How are you a single person? Aren't there people dying all over the world?"

He lifted one black eyebrow. "Not all of them require my personal attention."

That didn't answer anything. She demanded, "Wh-why do you look like Dragos? And why are you here, talking to me?"

"Come on now," he chided. "Catch up. You of all people should know how closely related death and the dragon are. As for why I'm here… that will become apparent soon enough. You're going to have to make some unpleasant choices, and a lot is going to hinge on the things that you and others do next."

"Pia!" Eva's sharp voice jolted her into looking. The other woman had walked to the edge of the stage and was looking up at her. "Nobody's here. What do you want to do?"

"That's not true, I was just…" Her voice trailed away as she realized the man who had been standing beside her had disappeared.

"You were just what?" Eva looked concerned. "What's going on? You look like you were a million miles away."

She listened to the sound of her own breathing. It took a thousand years for her eyelids to close in a single blink.

What's going on? I was just talking to Death, who is apparently closely related to my husband. No big deal.

I didn't realize Dragos had any family other than his sentinels. It's not like Death has shown up for any of our holiday dinners or brought the kids presents.

Come on, Pia. Catch up.

Then finally, just as Eva was about to jump onto the stage, Pia seemed to snap into time and place. Regaining the use of her limbs, she rushed to the stairs.

"Never mind," she said. Explaining what had just happened would take too much time, and she wasn't prepared to put it into words. Not yet, and maybe not without a lot of alcohol involved. "We need to go back to the Bellagio."

"Sure." Eva sounded easygoing, but her gaze was sharp. "You okay? You look like you've seen a ghost."

"Maybe I have. I don't want to talk about it." All she knew for sure was that she needed to see Dragos.

They had only been together for a couple of years. They had a young marriage and relationship, and even though their eldest son Liam had gone off to college, that was because he was an intensely magical being who had sprung into existence with a speed reminiscent of the first generation of Elder Races. If he had been any other boy, he would still be a toddler.

Still, she and Dragos had faced more than their fair share of conflict over their short time together, enough times to make Pia ask more than once, just who have I mated with?

Now her question shifted.

It was no longer *who* had she mated with but *what*?

The need to connect with him was so intense she reached out telepathically. Most people with telepathy had a range of only ten or so feet, but Dragos's range covered a hundred miles.

Silence greeted her attempt. She had already forgotten what Eva had told her, that casinos dampened telepathy.

As they left the lounge and strode through the gambling floor of the Riverview, a tall, dark man walked with them.

Death said, "Call on me anytime you want. Consider me at your disposal for the near future."

She felt her eyes strain as she looked around. There was nobody walking alongside her. Nobody but Eva, who was walking a little too close. There was an edge to Eva's jawline that said she was not as relaxed as she tried to appear.

Pia heard herself say, "I don't think I'm okay."

Eva's reaction was immediate and warm. Putting her arm around Pia, she said strongly, "You will be. Soon as we get into a cab, I'm going to call the doctor. And Dragos. Everything is going to be all right, honey."

Eva thought she meant physically, and Pia didn't attempt to correct her. Maybe there was something physically wrong and she had hallucinated what had just happened. Or maybe there was a perfectly reasonable explanation for it. As they approached the main doors of the casino, she allowed herself to believe everything really would be okay.

Until several people strode through the main doors and approached them.

The leader was a tall, powerfully built Elven woman. A jagged white scar split her splendid features. She was accompanied by six soldier types, all of them wearing flak jackets and weapons.

"I really don't like this," Eva muttered under her

breath. "Okay, Pia, *back up now* onto the gambling floor. We need to flag security."

Pia moved to obey, feeling as though she were swimming through mud. Whatever this impending confrontation was about, she and Eva weren't going to escape it. Out of the corner of her eye, she caught sight of the logo on the nearest soldier type. DEVIL'S GATE SECURITY.

Quickly the soldier types fanned out until she and Eva were surrounded. Smiling, the Elven woman said, "Pia Cuelebre? Oh, look how pregnant you are. That's just precious. My day keeps getting better and better."

Moving so fast she blurred, Eva pulled her Glock and aimed for the Elven woman's head. "Back up, asshole."

Instantly the soldiers that surrounded them pulled their weapons too, all aiming at Eva. Dread drove like a spike into Pia's chest. They weren't bluffing.

"Eva," Pia whispered, "put your gun down."

"Not a chance." Eva's expression had turned ruthless. She bared her teeth at the Elven woman. "You want to go there? Let's all go at once. They shoot me, I shoot you. Sure, I'll be dead, but so will you. I don't know who you are, and I don't give a shit. We're backing up onto the gambling floor, so get yourself out of my face."

"We don't have time for suicidal heroics," the Elven woman said. Her gaze switched to Pia, and her smile widened. She said to the soldiers, "Holster your weapons."

They did. Pia glanced quickly around. They stood at attention, watching the Elven woman, who said to Pia, "There, see? We're not going to have any violence here, only choices."

Choices – just as Azrael had warned. Pia's heart pounded harder.

Ignoring Eva, who had not lowered her gun, the woman held out a phone to Pia as she strode closer. "I've taken a friend of yours, Carling Severan. Here, you can see her for yourself."

She hadn't thought she could feel more fear than she already did, but it spiked again. Dragging her gaze from the Elf's face, she looked at the phone's screen.

The scene was no static photo. It was live footage. She stared at the beautiful unconscious woman sprawled on the desert ground. It was indisputably Carling, her short auburn hair tousled. She was bound with strands of what looked like shining silver wire, and a silver arrow protruded from her chest.

There were at least two people with Carling. One stood visible from the waist down, holding a crossbow pointed at Carling's head, while the other unseen person held the phone that filmed the scene.

"If you don't come with me right now," the Elven woman said softly, "he's going to shoot. Are you going to save Carling's life, or are you going to watch her die?"

No ordinary arrow would bring down a Vampyre of Carling's age and strength, nor would ordinary silver bind her. Carling was one of the most powerful sorceresses in the world, yet this woman had captured her.

And Rune was mated to her, indisputably mated for life. Their Las Vegas wedding was nothing more than putting icing on the proverbial cake. If Carling died, Rune died. It was as simple as that.

Pia looked up to meet the Elven woman's fearless, tigerish gaze. The Elf was a dead woman, of course, but some pretty important questions still remained. How would she die and how many casualties would she take down with her when she did?

Pia told her, "Of course I'll come."

"No," Eva snapped, tightening her arm around Pia's shoulders. "*No, you will not!*"

Even as she protested, one of the soldiers walked up to slam the butt of his gun into the side of her head. Eva dropped like a stone.

"Okay, maybe we'll have just a little violence," the Elven woman said, hitching one shoulder up in a quick shrug. She said into her phone, "Don't shoot her yet. Drain her so she'll be weakened if she wakes up."

As Pia tried to drop to her knees to check on Eva, two of the soldier types grabbed her arms, forcing her to remain on her feet. She wanted to scream in fury.

Instead, she said as steadily as she could, "This is not going to go well for you."

The Elven woman laughed. "We'll see how well it goes. When in Vegas you just have to roll the dice, know what I mean? Get to the roof," she said to the others. "Move it!"

The roof. That meant they had a helicopter waiting. Pia hadn't thought her heart could sink any further, but it did.

As they marched to a bank of elevators, she looked behind her. A couple of people were running over to Eva's crumpled figure. One of them stood and shouted for help, and uniformed security guards appeared on the scene. As the elevator doors closed, the last thing she saw was one of the casino guards talking into a walkie-talkie.

The entire confrontation had taken a minute or less, and none of the guards had yet realized a kidnapping was in progress.

Pia looked at the logo on one of her kidnapper's jackets. She asked, "What's in Devil's Gate?"

The Elven woman replied, "Your future."

Chapter Three

ARYAL'S ARGUMENT WITH New York's commissioner of development escalated to Dragos talking to the mayor in a conversation that spun into excruciating politeness.

In the past, the mayor had always been accommodating to Dragos's initiatives, even eager to please. But his reluctance to publicly partner with Cuelebre Enterprises on the construction of the proposed new sports stadium spoke volumes.

The mayor wasn't an especially strong-minded personality, but as a career politician he was a decent weather vane. He always turned in the direction the wind was blowing, and lately the wind had not been blowing in favor of the Elder Races.

Never mind that the stadium would draw in a great deal of money from both sports and entertainment events. The political climate for interactions between humans and the Elder Races had grown cold and unfriendly.

Finally Dragos told him, "We need to table this discussion for now. I have other things that need my attention."

"Certainly," the mayor said with thinly disguised relief. "And I have a meeting I need to step into. Perhaps we can look at this at a later date and see if there is a group of human investors we can bring to the table."

Dragos did not bother with pleasantries. Instead, he punched the End Call button, then handed the phone back to Aryal. "Scuttle the project," he told her. "I'm done."

He listened to what he had just said. *I'm done.* That had a ring of finality to it, and it felt like it covered a lot more than just the sports stadium. But he didn't have time to think about that.

Aryal made a face. "You sure? You sank a lot of money into the plans."

"I don't care."

She shrugged. "Can't say I'm surprised. It was doomed from the moment you gave it to me. You know my skills are investigative. I don't have the patience for this kind of political crap."

Dragos did know, but all his sentinels were overseeing areas outside their expertise as they covered the space left from Constantine's death. He would have already selected a seventh sentinel except that his son, Liam, had begged him for a year to prepare for the chance to compete for the position. Against his better judgment, he had agreed.

"It's a moot point now," he said shortly. "So forget about it."

The truth was, his heart had never been fully committed to the project. He had pursued it because on paper it looked like a lucrative opportunity, but in reality, his instincts were pulling him in another direction entirely.

He had far more interest in his building plans for a new community in the Other land that was connected by crossover passageways to upstate New York. He had started that project to create a bolt-hole for the Wyr demesne in case relations between humankind and the Elder Races grew too strained, but what had begun as a contingency plan had quickly become an obsession.

Lately his thoughts kept returning more and more to that vast stretch of virgin territory. For an Other land it was immense, roughly the size of Greenland. He had sent expedition parties out twice, and so far they had only found three crossover passageways that connected to Earth and Other lands.

Just thinking of that place held a sense of freedom and opportunity he hadn't experienced in a very long time. But instead of focusing on that, he had turned his attention to the stadium project.

He couldn't shake the feeling that he'd been doing a lot of things wrong lately, following old habits and patterns. Working on the wrong things, missing vital cues. Saying the wrong things. He scowled up at the billboard Pia had pointed out to him earlier, then glanced around. Their entourage had disappeared several minutes ago.

"Now that that excruciating piece of business is over with, I'm going to track Rune down," Aryal said. "I feel an intense need to give him a noogie. Plus we've got to decide where we're going for his bachelor's party after dinner."

"Text me when you decide," he said. "I'm going to our suite."

She stuck her thumb up. As they headed in separate directions, wrongness snapped at Dragos's heels.

He's nobody. Ignore him. *Wrong reply.*

You're so big you actually need my help this time. *Wrong thing to say.*

He hadn't needed to see the hurt that had darkened Pia's eyes to know that had been wrong. He had felt it as soon as it had come out of his mouth. She *was* so big she actually needed his help, and in fact she'd been making jokes about that herself.

But while Dragos would never win prizes for his insight into feminine outlook and behavior, he was beginning to suspect her self-deprecating jokes weren't really jokes at all but an attempt to mask something that ran much deeper. This pregnancy was wearing on her—it was wearing on them both.

He wanted to growl and bite somebody's head off. He wanted to savage the sense of wrongness at his heels, but it didn't have a physical body. And he needed to put his arms around her and apologize for being an insensitive ass. To kiss her neck and feel her lean back against him and rub his face in her hair.

As he let himself into their suite, the first thing he noticed was the sense of emptiness inside. There was a white folded paper on the hall table. He picked it up.

Gone sightseeing. I'll be back in a little bit. Have fun with Rune. :) Love you, P.

As he read it, he fingered one corner, eyes narrowed in thought. Why had she written a note instead of texting? Lifting the paper, he inhaled. It smelled like her, which was also wrong. The drug she had to take daily to save their baby's life had changed her body chemistry.

Carefully, he folded the note and tucked it in his pocket while he reached out to her telepathically. No connection. Since they were in Vegas, that wasn't terribly surprising. Still, he never liked having any of his abilities or inclinations curbed.

Pulling out his phone, he texted, What did you decide to do, and when will you be back? And after pausing, he added, Also, I'm an ass, and I'm sorry.

Then, while he waited for her to notice his text and respond, he strode out of the suite and went to join Rune and the others.

He found them in one of the Bellagio's luxurious private gambling rooms. Aryal texted the information to him as he reached the elevator. When he strode into the room, he found Rune, Aryal, Claudia, Luis, and Duncan sitting at the poker table.

Three beautiful women were in attendance, two of whom hung on Rune's shoulders while the third woman acted as dealer. Duncan's fiancée, Seremela, sat beside him, although she didn't participate in the game.

Everyone hailed Dragos cheerfully. Amusement suffused their faces. Dragos studied Rune's handsome features. The gryphon's hair was mussed as though someone had been running their fingers through it, and his skin was darkened—it looked like he was… blushing?

"Really, there is no need," he said forcefully to the grinning women draped over him. "You are both very beautiful. Whatever she paid you, I will double it if you stop."

Aryal and Seremela laughed harder.

"Oh honey," Aryal cooed at the closest woman. "That's okay if he doesn't want you. I do. My mate is all the way back in New York, and my lap is lonely."

Dragos suppressed a smile. "What's going on?"

"You don't even want to know," Rune muttered.

"Yes, I do." Dragos stuck his hands in his pockets and rocked back on his heels while he waited for the explanation.

"Well, I don't want to talk about it." As Rune spoke, one of the women draped her arm around his neck. He pulled it off again and said to her, "What are you, an octopus? How many arms do you have—and where were you when I was unmated?"

Chuckling, Duncan said to Dragos, "Carling and Rune traveled separately. She got in last night."

"We're staying in separate suites too until after the wedding," Rune said, frustration evident in his voice.

"Although I don't know why I agreed to that.... Ladies, come on!"

"You agreed because you thought a little abstinence would be sexy, but now you're regretting it." Aryal snickered. She told Dragos, "Carling set some booby traps for Rune before she went to bed. Literally, get it? Boob-y traps, ar ar ar. She paid all the single female servers to fawn over him. Whenever he goes anywhere, he gets mobbed by beautiful women."

"I've been hiding in here playing poker ever since," Rune said. His face was lit, and he looked happier than Dragos had ever seen him. He had to give Carling credit for that—she knew how to keep Rune's cat nature amused.

Dragos said, "Want me to sit in for you?"

"No, no! That's okay!" Everybody responded at once.

"Nobody ever wants to play poker with me," he murmured as he checked his phone. No reply yet. "A pity—it's my favorite game."

The dealer told him, "Carling is hosting a roulette table in here. Of course, your gambling ban applies to anywhere else in the Bellagio and in Las Vegas, but in this room, you're welcome to play roulette if you like."

"No, thanks," Dragos told her. Games with dice and rolling balls held no interest for him. Blackjack was okay in a pinch. No, he liked the math and the strategy involved in poker, the experience of looking into his opponents' eyes and assessing their game—and then beating them. "I'll watch the card game instead."

Within a few hands, he had the probabilities sketched out. When one of the women peeled off Rune to serve everyone drinks, he ordered a scotch and checked his phone again. Still no reply.

A light bulb went off inside his capacious mind.

That was why she had written the note instead of texting him earlier. She had wanted to put some distance between them. She hadn't wanted him to respond right away, and if she had texted he would have.

Was that why she hadn't told him where she had gone?

He's nobody. Ignore him.

Ah, of course. The light bulb got brighter. She hadn't told him where she was going because she knew he wouldn't approve. He had shut her down on the subject after all.

"Goddamn it," he said abruptly, and the banter around the poker table paused. He tossed back his scotch. "I need to step out."

"Want some company?" Aryal asked. She had coaxed one of the women onto her lap and looked as relaxed as the others.

"No," he told her. "You're not on duty. Stay and enjoy yourself."

"Duty schmuty." The harpy gave a casual shrug, but her gray eyes were sharply attentive. "Call or text if you need me."

Aryal was a lunatic, of course, and she had the social

skills of a buzz saw, but her instincts were as sensitive as butterfly antenna. He had always appreciated that about her.

"Goes for both of us," Rune murmured.

Dragos dropped a hand on Aryal's shoulder and gave Rune a nod. "Will do."

As he strode out and made his way through the labyrinthine casino, his mood grew blacker.

What else had he expected Pia to do? She had done what he would have done, the most logical thing. When she couldn't get an answer out of him, she had gone to find answers for herself.

As he stepped outside the main entrance, his phone pinged. He snatched at it.

The text was from Pia.

Of course you're an ass. You've always been an ass. You're a murderous monstrosity that should have been hunted down and exterminated centuries ago.

What. The. Fuck.

Dragos stopped dead as he stared at the small screen. That text wasn't from Pia. A new landscaped unfurled in front of him, and in it everything was scorched black.

Rapidly he texted back. Where is my wife?

His phone pinged again almost immediately. Wife. LOL, isn't that cute? Beasts don't marry. They mate. They spawn. They make more monsters like themselves unless they're stopped.

He punched the Call button, but all it did was ring. His hands shook and talons sprang out, and his heartbeat thundered in his ears so that he had difficulty typing out another text when all he wanted to do was crush the phone into powder, but his phone might be the only link he had to Pia.

And if this stranger had Pia's phone, she might already be dead.

Wouldn't he feel it if she had been killed? Wouldn't he know something? He thought of the man on the billboard, and convulsive tremors ran through his muscles.

What do you want? He managed to finish and hit Send.

Again, his phone pinged right away. Good boy. Pat, pat. Now sit! Stay! And keep your phone with you. I'll let you know what I want soon. Here's proof of life. She looks tired. I don't think you've been good for her. Or maybe that's the monster pup she's trying to whelp.

The photo was of Pia, standing on a pavement out in the sunshine. She wasn't restrained or injured in any way that Dragos could see. She simply stood looking at the camera, arms wrapped around herself, her expression clenched and sober. Dark shadows circled her eyes.

She did look tired.

Instinctively he tried again to reach out telepathically. *Pia? Goddamn it, PIA, ANSWER ME!*

There was no response.

His phone remained silent.

An agonized rage welled up inside. Like the birth of a tidal wave, it couldn't be stopped. He had to release it.

Throwing back his head, the dragon roared.

Chapter Four

O VERHEAD, GLASS FROM the ornate portico shattered, and the cavernous sound of over-stressed steel and concrete filled his ears along with other screams. Car alarms went off, adding to the cacophony.

When he opened his eyes again, he looked down at the panicked creatures below him as they ran away. He had shapeshifted without realizing it. He had never gone through an uncontrolled shapeshift before.

Concrete pillars lay broken around him like so many toys, and the bent weight of the portico lay across his back. The Bellagio itself had cracks running up the side, as did the nearby buildings. All of them had broken windows.

Several people exploded out of the rubble of the doors. Rune and Aryal shapeshifted as they ran, and Seremela, Claudia, and Luis followed on their heels, while Duncan stood back in the shadows. As a Vampyre, he couldn't step outside without protection. In an eyeblink, Dragos took in everyone's presence, then dismissed them.

The gryphon and the harpy landed beside him, both

looking wild.

Flames licked out of the dragon's mouth as he hissed, "Pia's been kidnapped."

Shock held them frozen, and then the gryphon roared and the harpy shrieked. They had their own rage. One of their own had been taken.

Ignoring the chaos he had caused, Dragos looked from them to the others. "Organize. Investigate." Those were all the words he could manage past the fury and terror burning in his chest.

"Grace and Khalil haven't arrived yet," Luis said. "I'll call them and get them here right away."

Aryal added, "Neither are Bayne, Graydon, and Beluviel. Get that Djinn to transport them here—and if he bargains for a favor, I'll ram one down his throat!"

"I'll handle it," Luis said. He had partially shifted too, his face monstrous and hands ready for killing.

"I'll wake Carling." Rune launched and winged toward the Spa Tower.

Aryal asked, "Has anybody heard from Eva?"

"No. She might be dead." Dragos couldn't hold back any longer. Shrugging off the steel that trapped him, he snarled, "I need to hunt."

Lunging into the air, he winged toward the Riverview Casino, and the harpy followed closely behind. He might not know where Pia's kidnappers had taken her, but he knew where she had gone.

Were taking her. Were. They hadn't had Pia long, because Pia hadn't been gone long. The photo had been of Pia standing on a pavement somewhere. The scene hadn't had any identifying characteristics, but concrete was a city concept. *She was close.* He knew it in his bones. He just had to get to her before the kidnappers had a chance to really disappear.

He reached out again to her telepathically. *Pia. Come on, lover, answer me.*

Nothing. Goddamn Vegas with the goddamn magic dampeners all over the goddamn place. *Aryal!* he roared. *Get the gaming commission to have all the casinos on the strip lift their magic restrictions! Don't let them argue about how much that will cost or how it will shut down the casino floors—I already know, and I will reimburse them. Money is no object.*

I'm on it!

As she wheeled away, Rune's roar filled his mind. *Carling is gone!*

Dragos eased up on his headlong flight as he absorbed the news. *What do you mean, gone?*

MY MATE IS MISSING! Rune's agonized fury tore through his head. *All her things are in her room, but she hasn't slept in her bed—she's gone! I can't find her anywhere!*

Thoughts like spears of lightning blasted through Dragos's mind. Nearly every hotel of size had Vampyrefriendly rooms. While some were located in the basement, others had safety shutters that closed at daybreak.

Aside from that, they were normal hotel rooms like any other... It was up to individual Vampyres and their attendants to take added security measures if they wished. Carling had almost certainly warded her surroundings. Maybe she had taken other precautions.

He said, *Was her room broken into?*

No! Not that I can tell. There are other scents here, but they could be hotel staff. Rune sounded savage and impatient, as if words had become so intolerable he needed to leap ahead to another state of being. Dragos could relate. *I didn't get here until almost noon. She might have been missing for hours, and I never knew. She'd wanted to travel ahead to take care of wedding arrangements.*

Pia had been kidnapped, and Carling was missing...

Dragos growled, *This is no coincidence. Have you heard from anybody yet?*

No. No text, no phone call or note—not a fucking thing. Claudia and Luis came with her. They said when they left her, she was safely in her suite. I'm trying to track her now. Duncan's interviewing Bellagio security.

Tracking someone in a resort of the Bellagio's fame and size would be a nightmare. The casino floors were massive, and they had thousands of rooms. While not all the rooms would be occupied at once, not all the visitors would be staying overnight in the hotel either. There were literally thousands of random scents, crisscrossing and overlaid on each other.

Dragos ground his teeth. *Keep me posted.*

As they finished speaking, Dragos could see the Riverview Casino's signature rooftop garden and helipad ahead. A fire engine, ambulance, and several police cars were parked at the front entrance where a sizable crowd had gathered.

Ah. That looked like a sizable bread crumb. The casino had seen some trouble.

People screamed and scattered as he plummeted toward them. He had forgotten to cloak his presence. Shapeshifting, he raced over to the nearest police officer, a woman, who turned white and backed up several steps before making herself stop.

"My wife has been kidnapped," he growled. "What happened here?"

Swallowing hard, the policewoman said, "I'm very s-sorry to hear that, my lord. We heard your r—We heard you. We have an unconscious woman who sustained a blow to the head and several eyewitness accounts of a group of people walking away from her. Preliminary statements are inconsistent and confused. We're about to review the casino security tapes to see what happened...."

He stopped listening. Running over to the ambulance, he looked in the back. Eva's unconscious figure was strapped to a gurney. With her was a paramedic, who said, "You can't be here, sir—"

Blood had leaked out of Eva's nostrils and the corner of one eye. Somebody had hit her hard. Baring his teeth, he growled at the paramedic. "Don't tell me where I can and cannot be. She's one of my mine. Will she live?"

The paramedic had cringed back, but he answered quickly. "She has a serious skull fracture. We need to get her to the hospital. Prompt treatment will vastly increase her chances of survival."

"Go." He left the ambulance and raced into the casino. There were too many people milling about, too many... along with a thin, subtle thread of Pia's scent. It held him transfixed. Following her scent would be a chancy business in this crowd of gawkers. The Riverview wasn't quite as large as the Bellagio, but it was large enough.

He might get better information more quickly if he tracked down the Midnight Lounge.

He pushed through the crowd, looking for the lounge. The number of people milling about heightened the sense of savagery burning through his body. He needed them to back off or, better yet, leave. With each step he had to consciously control the feral instinct to burn them all where they stood.

A couple of uniformed security people approached at a rapid pace. They were Light Fae, and they wore the Riverview's signature colors.

"My lord," said one male. "We've heard you caused significant damage to the Bellagio. We don't want any trouble—I'm going to have to ask you to leave."

Dragos rounded on him. Both security turned white. "You don't want any trouble," he repeated very quietly. "You've already got trouble. My wife was here. One of my people—her bodyguard—was attacked here. She's on her way to the hospital, and my wife has been kidnapped. Presumably, I believe, from here."

The security guard went even whiter. He swallowed.

"I'm so sorry—we didn't realize you were involved in this. We're still piecing together what happened."

Dragos said between his teeth, "Piece it together faster. Blonde woman. You might have seen her in the news. She and her bodyguard came through here."

The other guard said, "The security footage shows a blonde woman with a group walking away from the victim. That could be Lady Cuelebre. They got on an elevator over there." He pointed. "We're still scouring the whole building, but we believe they've left."

Dragos considered the bank of elevators. "Where do those lead?"

"Well... everywhere," the second guard said. "They go all the way up to the roof and down several levels to the parking garage below."

The roof. Sunshine. Pavement.

And the Riverview had a helipad.

They might have left by car. But if they took her airborne, they could be fifty miles away by now, or more. And the distance would be growing every minute.

The distance itself was an issue he could overcome, but he couldn't if he didn't know which direction they had flown in, and the skies around Las Vegas were full of helicopters and small pleasure aircraft.

"Get me the list of everyone who requested permission to use your helipad today," he said abruptly. "I want you to email it to my cell phone as fast as you can. Got it?"

"Yes, sir," the older guard said. He took down the

number. "I'll see to this immediately. Is there anything else?"

"Yes. Who is playing at the Midnight Lounge?"

If the seemingly random question surprised the other male, he didn't show it. He said, "One of the magicians that makes the Vegas circuit from the time to time—Rael Malweth. But I think his show ended today."

It ended? Today?

He realized he was breathing rapidly and opening and closing his hands to keep from grabbing the guard by the throat. Both men watched him warily, poised as if to run. Not that running would do them any good if Dragos chose to lunge for them.

He forced himself to say, "Thank you."

Both guards reacted as if he had released them from prison, retreating rapidly. The one promised, "I'll fax you that list right away, my lord!"

"Be sure you do," he said. "Don't make me come find you."

As he turned away, he noticed how many people were watching them. They shrank away as his gaze passed over them.

In the back of his mind, he knew his actions were going to have consequences from the damage to the Bellagio and the rest of the city, and the fear he was engendering in everyone who saw him.

The cost alone of closing down all the casinos on the strip would probably run over twenty million dollars a day, maybe more. The general public loved Pia, which might mitigate some things a bit, but not much.

When he'd found out Pia was missing, he should have gone into stealth mode and attacked the issue quietly. He was doing damage everywhere he went, but he didn't care. He didn't care. He would happily burn the whole city to the ground, if only it would bring her back unharmed.

But damage to the city, and to human and Elder Races relations, might also be what the kidnappers had intended. He remembered the last time he had lost control of his rage and roared in New York, when he had discovered his hoard had been broken into. There had been quite a bit of PR work needed to clean up that mess.

Snapping his fingers at the onlookers, he said, "Somebody film me."

Instantly several people pointed their cell phones at him. Turning in a slow circle, he said, "I damaged this city, which I regret, and I will make full restitution to Las Vegas for it. My wife, Pia Cuelebre, has been kidnapped. I'm offering five-million-dollar rewards for any substantial, verifiable information that will lead to her recovery. That's not just one reward—that's as many five-million-dollar rewards as it takes to get my wife back alive. The Wyr demesne in New York has a crime hotline number." He rattled off the digits. "If you have any information about Pia's whereabouts, call that number now. Help me get my wife and our unborn child back safely."

After that, he made a slicing motion with one hand. As those who had been filming him lowered their phones, he counted them. There were twelve in total, and while they still watched him with wariness and fear, now there was a good deal more understanding, even sympathy, in their expressions.

"Upload your clips to social media," he told them. "Call newspapers and TV stations and offer it to them. I will pay you for every outlet you get that out on—and the bigger the outlet is, the more money you'll get. Fifty thousand for national coverage. Twenty-five thousand for local. I'll pay each of you a thousand if you upload it to your Facebook and Twitter accounts and make this turn viral. Go!"

Everyone scattered, all except one young woman who walked up to him. She said quietly, "I'll do it for free. I hope you find her."

She was human. She was nobody. But as he looked into her compassionate gaze, the fiery rage in his chest died down until, for a moment, all he felt was raw pain.

"Thank you," he said.

She nodded.

With the next pulse beat, he was on fire again and moving. It would be a simple matter to go up to the rooftop and see if he could catch Pia's scent and quicker to fly up rather than take the elevator. Once outside, he cloaked himself, shapeshifted, and launched.

As he soared upward, Aryal said, *Khalil transported the rest of the wedding party here. We've got thirteen people, two of*

*whom are doctors. Four are aerial fighters and sentinels—or at
least, you know, Rune used to be one—and Khalil said he will
take anybody anywhere they need to go. And the gaming
commission is working with the casinos for a citywide shutdown.
Should be happening any minute now. Grace is trying her Oracle
woo-woo stuff to see if she can see anything that way. What have
you got?*

While she talked, Dragos landed on the helipad. As
soon as he did, he caught Pia's scent along with several
others. Shapeshifting back into his human form, he knelt
to get closer to the scents.

A few of them seemed tantalizingly familiar. Inhaling
deeply, he tried to pin them down, but the memories
went back—far back. Try as he might to chase them
down, they eluded him for now.

They went airborne, he said. *I'm on the Riverview helipad
and Pia's scent is up here. And if they have enough magic to take
Carling, they have enough to cloak their presence. We've lost them.*

Aw, shit. Her reply was subdued. *Dragos, I'm so sorry.*

Shut up, he told her savagely. *We're going to find them.*

She flared in immediate response. *Of course we will!
And when we do, gods help them.*

Standing, he spun in a slow circle, looking out in all
directions at the endless blue sky.

I know you're there, he said, and this time he wasn't
trying to talk to Pia or Aryal. For the first time in many
centuries, he reached out, of his own volition, to
someone else. *The guard said your show here at the Riverview
has closed, but you haven't left. I can sense it.*

There was silence for so long Dragos thought he wasn't going to get a reply.

But then Azrael said, *You're right. I haven't left. Not yet, but soon.*

Dragos closed his hands into fists. *Where is she?*

Azrael appeared beside him. "I don't know yet," he told Dragos. "That means she is not close to dying. That is something."

Whirling, Dragos grabbed Azrael by the throat, teeth bared. "She came to see you."

Calm, ageless green eyes met his. "Yes."

"And you knew this was coming? You could have said something to stop it?" His talons dug into the other male's throat. All he would have to do to kill Azrael was clench his fist and tear out his throat. Azrael might be Death, but he was also a man.

But like all the other Primal Powers, Death couldn't be killed or stopped, only its current manifestation could. If Azrael died, another creature would either be born or rise up to take his place.

Azrael didn't struggle against his hold. "You know it doesn't work like that. The universe is predicated on free will and probability. Would she turn right or left? Would she fight her captors or capitulate? Maybe her captors would have a change in plans and lie in wait for her somewhere else. Maybe they would change their minds and go home, or maybe they would choose to attack you directly. And what is everybody else going to do? All those life choices are outside my realm, which is death, and we have not yet begun that dance, but somehow we will. That much I know. Somehow, my brother, we will."

"Don't call me that." Dragos threw him backward.

With inhuman grace, Azrael spun and righted himself. When he spoke next, a scythe had entered his voice. "And why not? That's what we were—what we are. You killed, and I took what you reaped. Then you turned from killing to living, but I didn't hold it against you. Like death, living is a necessary part of the Great Wheel. One cannot exist without the other. But what I don't understand is why do you deny that I am still a part of you?"

"I don't deny it!" he roared, spinning away while emotions so violent they felt cataclysmic crashed and tore at him. Then, more calmly, he said, "I don't deny it. But I am not the same beast I once was. Like you said, I have reached for life. I will not go back to that feral time."

"Not unless she dies," Azrael said gently. "And I can't save you from that particular pain if it were to happen, although if I could, I would."

Rubbing his face hard, Dragos fought to get himself under control. When he could speak again, he asked, "What do you know about Carling?"

When nothing but silence greeted him, he spun around again.

Azrael was gone. Dragos stood on the rooftop, alone.

Chapter Five

PIA WOKE IN stages. Her first thought was *Last Dance*, ha. Death's Vegas show was a little heavy-handed on the metaphor. Or was it a simile? She could never keep those two straight.

Her hip and neck hurt, and the baby was kicking at her full bladder. Why was the bed so hard, and who had put rocks in it?

Awareness came crashing in. Bolting into a sitting position, she looked around wildly. The last thing she remembered was sitting in a helicopter with her kidnappers. Most of them were just goons taking orders.

The one she was really afraid of was the Elven woman with the scarred face. Not since coming face-to-face with Urien had Pia looked in a person's gaze and realized they were capable of doing anything, anything at all.

Then, a sudden blackness. They must have hit her with some kind of spell.

And now this.

She was in a shallow cave that had been converted into a cell. Instead of being underground, it appeared to be some distance aboveground, possibly twenty or thirty feet up a cliff face. She could look out over a desertlike clearing that was surrounded by a dense, strange-looking forest. A multitude of colored dome tents and campers lined the edges of the clearing and disappeared past her line of sight.

The opening of the cave was barred with some sturdy metal beams that definitely meant business, and they were secured into place by what appeared to be newly poured concrete at the base. Outside, there was a narrow ledge about four feet wide.

There was no door set in the bars. There wasn't any way out that she could see.

Her stomach clenched. She wasn't meant to leave this place.

The only items in the cave were a bucket in the corner and a pile of cloth and leathery bones in another. The pressure against her bladder had become urgent, so she quickly used the bucket while her mind raced, cataloguing more details.

Sunshine poured in, warming half the ground inside the cave and leaving the rest in shadow. At the moment, the breeze that blew through the cave was hot and dry, but it would get cold at night.

She was wearing a sleeveless tunic that flared to comfortably accommodate her pregnant belly, ankle-length trousers, and flat sandals. The outfit was stylish enough for a casual sightseeing jaunt, but it wouldn't offer any warmth or protection when night fell.

Outside, the clearing was full of activity. Dozens of workers were constructing a large wooden structure that looked like a dragon. At the base, they stacked high piles of more wood.

The scene reminded her of articles she had read about the annual Burning Man festival held in the Nevada desert. The Burning Man festival was, by all accounts, a place for wild freedom of creative and personal expression. Although it had become better organized in recent years and had a security presence for the duration, it still held a touch of anarchy, and unpredictable things happened.

Were they building a giant effigy to burn? Of *Dragos*?

She pressed against the bars as she tried to see as much as she could, clenching her hands around two pieces of the round metal. In direct sunlight, they were too hot to hold for long, and the desert sun was too fierce for her pale skin, especially without any sunblock for protection.

Rubbing her belly anxiously, she backed away to the nearest strip of shadow at the back of the cave. Her heart hammered, and her skin felt clammy, and her mouth dry. She had no idea how long she had been unconscious, but as hungry and shaky as she felt, it could have been a full day.

That meant she needed to take a dose of the protocol, but there wasn't any to be had. She had a couple of emergency doses in her purse, but the Elven woman had taken that along with her cell phone.

As she came back alongside the pile of bones and rags, it moved.

"Pia," it whispered.

She nearly leaped out of her skin. What she had taken for a dead body was someone who was all too clearly alive—and whoever it was knew her.

Falling to her knees beside the person, she gently helped to shift them around. It felt like holding a bag of sticks in her arms. Horrified compassion washed over her as she stared down at the skeletal face.

The skin was stretched tight over the facial structure, making it look skull-like, unrecognizable. It wore clothes that were well-made and feminine, but they were falling off the bony body. That, together with the untidy shock of luxurious auburn hair, brought a sick realization.

She breathed, "Oh my God. Carling?"

The figure opened its eyes. They were red.

"I'm afraid so." The Vampyre's voice was weak and thready. She had become so desiccated she had lost all semblance of her famous beauty. Even the fullness of her lips was gone, which brought her extended fangs into prominence. "I'm sorry to see you here. I had hoped you might be someone I wouldn't care about."

Carefully Pia eased her against the wall and backed into the sunlight. If Carling had been human, she would have unquestionably been long dead. Only the fact that she was a Vampyre had kept her alive. Or as alive as the undead ever got. But the differences between this ruin of a figure and Carling's normal vitality and strength were terrible.

"I'm sorry to see you too," she whispered. "I heard one of them, the leader, give the order to drain you while you were unconscious. Is that what—what—"

"What caused this? Yes, it's severe exsanguination." With a dry sound like the rustle of bones, Carling shifted against the cave wall. "It's an effective method for weakening a Powerful Vampyre to keep them under control. It's also an effective method of torture. With the exsanguination, the sun, and the spelled bars, they could hold me here indefinitely. How did they get you?"

Pia told her about the confrontation at the Riverview. "I'm worried about Eva. They hit her really hard." She paused. "How did they get you?"

"They shot me. I'd said good night to Claudia and Luis, but then I'd gotten a message that a package from Rune was waiting for me at the front desk." She shook her head in disgust. "I didn't want to leave my room so close to morning, but I also didn't want to wait to see what he had sent me, so I had them deliver it. When I opened my door, they tagged me with a silver arrow that was spelled with something. They have a very good magic user."

"Ah yes, that would be me."

The voice came from behind Pia. She spun around to stare at the scarred Elven woman who stood on the other side of the bars along with another Elf who carried a tray.

The Elven woman held a crossbow pointed at Pia's

belly. The woman was shaking and tears ran down her grimacing face.

"After all these centuries," she said. "After watching that horrible dragon prosper and gather power for so long, right now all I have to do to kill him is shoot you. I can't tell you how wonderful that feels. I hold his life in my hands. So you see, I'm torn. Do I feed you or do I pull the trigger?"

Slowly Pia backed up until she stood flattened against the cave wall. Carling rose to stand beside her.

Carling said, "Take a moment to think. You don't want to do this."

Laughter burst out explosively from the woman. "You have no idea how much I want to do this. That monster killed everybody I loved!"

Everyone? Pia didn't have to know the details to recognize the other woman was telling the truth. Either Dragos had gone to war, or the Elves had. Their hatred for each other had lasted for eons. This was a wound from one of those ancient battles, and it had never healed.

There was nowhere to go, and nothing she could do except talk. She didn't bother trying to convince the Elven woman that Dragos had evolved and changed. Looking into that implacable face, she knew the other woman would never listen.

Forcing herself to remain steady, she said as calmly as she could, "When my father died, my mother lived for sixteen more years. I don't think this is going to get you the results that you want. I can see how badly you want my mate to die, but he may simply choose not to, for as long as his will can hold him here. And if there's one thing I think we can all agree on, Dragos has an indomitable will."

The Elven woman pulled the trigger.

And that was it, that was it. For one hellish split second, Pia knew she and the baby were dead. She didn't even have time to draw in a breath to scream.

But in the same moment, Carling blurred beside her, and suddenly the Vampyre was clasping the arrow. Frozen, Pia stared into Carling's fierce red gaze, just inches from her own. Carling had just saved her life. Had saved Stinkpot.

Then the Elven woman wiped her face and laughed. "I guess that's enough of a decision for now. You have more strength than I had expected, Carling Severan. You should be a useless pile in the corner."

"Clearly you know who we are," Carling said. "Who are you?"

"I am Caerlovena. I rule this place and everyone in it." She gestured to her companion, and he slipped the tray through a slot in the bars. She said to Carling, "When I heard you were coming to Las Vegas, I knew I had to capture you somehow. I had waited so long to get this kind of chance. If I held your life over his head, I could force your Wyr to kill Dragos—and he would have. The Wyr will do anything to protect their mates." Her tigerish gaze shifted back to Pia, and she bared her teeth in a ferocious facsimile of a smile. "But then I heard you were attending their wedding, and *that* opportunity seemed too good to be true, if I could only find a way to take you too. Now, one way or another, I know he's going to die. I just want to know how much pain I can make him suffer before he does. And I really want him to suffer, so it's just as well you stopped me from killing her."

"Okay," Pia said. Halfway through Crazy Elf's speech, her head had started to pound. She could feel her heartbeat racing too fast, and a watery weakness filled her limbs. "Things are bad, and they are going to get worse. Got it. Can I have my purse, please?"

"What?" Caerlovena stared at her with baffled contempt, as if she couldn't quite believe what she had heard.

Gritting her teeth, Pia repeated, "Can I have my purse, please?"

The Elven woman didn't bother to reply. She said to Carling, "Sooner or later, the blood thirst is going to take you. Enjoy your time with each other."

She strode away, followed by the other Elf.

"That was staggeringly awful," Pia said.

Carling looked down at the arrow she still held. "It could have gone worse."

The world began to spin. Moving unsteadily over to the wall, Pia used it to help her ease to a sitting position. She lost track of the world around her as it faded into a formless white, but then she came alert with a jerk as

Carling knelt beside her.

Heart pounding, she shrank back. Looking into the Vampyre's face was like looking into a nightmare. But, she noticed, while Carling's eyes might be red, they were also calm.

She managed to make her rubbery lips shape words. "How bad is the blood thirst?" Carling looked so terrible it had to be bad.

Carling put her hand on Pia's shoulder. "Listen to me," she said. "Caerlovena is wrong. I have been starving before. I have been tortured, and I survived. I can survive the blood thirst as well. I will not let her take away my choices or my sense of self. You are safe with me, Pia."

She nodded. She could tell that Carling wanted her to believe it, and she did, up to a point, but they might have another conversation entirely if she went into labor. Giving birth was a messy business. How would Carling deal with the blood if that happened?

"I really needed my purse," she said.

"You need a drink, but unfortunately I can't help you with that." Carling looked at the tray where it sat in sunlight. "And your pulse is far too thready and fast for my liking. You have to get that tray. Can you do that?"

She shook her head. "Maybe in a minute."

Carling eased down beside her, keeping one bony finger on the vein at the inside her wrist. Pia allowed it. A listlessness was washing over her.

She roused herself to say, "You know they're tearing

apart Las Vegas to find us."

"I know. Unfortunately, we're not in Las Vegas." The Vampyre tapped her finger on Pia's wrist. "Caerlovena. I know that name."

"Her goons," Pia said thickly. Her tongue felt funny and kind of swollen.

Carling's skull face frowned at her. "What about her goons?"

"They had logos on their chests. *Devil's Gate Security.*"

Carling snapped her twiggy fingers. "That's where we're at. Devil's Gate. Duncan and Seremela came here once to rescue Seremela's niece, back when the Djinn Malphas was still alive. They said there were a number of dangerous power brokers here at the time, and Caerlovena was one of them. She must have either taken out the other power brokers or driven them away. Did you see how twisted the vegetation is at the edge of the clearing? I think she's trying to create an Elven forest in the desert. I've heard there is no better warning system than an Elven forest that is awake, aware, and attuned to you, but this isn't the right climate for that kind of land magic. She must be straining the land's resources for miles around."

"I don't care," Pia said simply. Leaning her head back against the wall, she closed her eyes. "Do you know what I care about? I care that Dragos and I have been fighting the past couple of weeks, and those are the last things we may be able to say to each other."

She waited for Carling to reassure her, to tell her that

of course everything was going to be all right, but the Vampyre didn't.

Instead, after a moment Carling asked, "What have you been fighting about?"

"A couple of weeks ago, Stinkpot—that's our nickname for the baby—became viable. We were so happy we had a viability party, just the two of us. But now Dragos wants me to induce labor, and I told him no. The baby might be viable, but that doesn't mean he's ready to be born yet. If he was ready, he'd let us know— he'd already be here. I'm going to hold on to him for every minute I possibly can, and he will be safer, stronger, and healthier because of it."

Carling said gently, "This pregnancy is hard on you."

"Of course it is." She made a face. "It has fucked me up, and Dragos hates that. I can feel him watching me. I know what he's doing, and I know how he thinks. To him, it's measuring one statistic against another. If the baby's viable, then it's less danger and hardship on me to induce, and then we all win. But I don't see it that way." A tear slipped out of the corner of her eye. "The thing is, neither one of us is necessarily wrong... except I'm right. We just needed to stop fighting about it."

"He does not handle opposition well," Carling said dryly. "I'm no soothsayer, but I'll guess this isn't going to be the last time you and he argue."

A small snort escaped Pia. "Probably not. I'm a lot more easygoing than he is, so usually we make things work without too much fuss. I think it has surprised him how adamantly I've dug in my heels over this."

"Well, take heart," Carling told her. "The sun has just gone behind a cloud, so I'm going to get that tray while I can, and you're going to drink some water."

Pia watched her shuffle over to the tray and drag it back across the cave floor. Carling's brief burst of speed and energy were a thing of the past. Now she moved like a very old, sick woman.

The tray held a plastic jug of water, warm from the sunlight, an apple, and some kind of meat sandwich. Ignoring the sandwich, Pia drank half the water, until her thirst was sated. Then she inhaled the apple, core and all. It wasn't enough food, but at least it was something.

"You should eat the sandwich too," Carling told her when she was finished.

She shook her head. "Not if I want to keep that apple down. There's meat in it. Just the smell is making me queasy."

"Not even the bread?"

She grimaced. "Meat juice."

"Okay, well, it's better than it was. And there's another thing."

"What's that?"

The Vampyre held up the arrow. "We have one more tool than we did a little while ago, and it's got a strong metal tip." She narrowed her eyes at the bars. "That concrete is fresh enough maybe I can scrape at the base of those bars and weaken them."

She thought of the slow, old-woman way Carling had

shuffled across the cave. The Vampyre hadn't even been able to lift the tray. She sighed. "You need to drink too."

The Vampyre's red gaze and terrifying visage turned back to her. Carling said softly, "I can't do that."

"You have to. Right now you can barely stand upright on your own." Pia injected strength into her voice. "I have a lot of blood right now because of the pregnancy. If you take a little, it's not going to put me into labor."

No, Pia was going to do that all on her own. Without the protocol to dampen her immune system, her body was going to start rejecting the baby.

You'd better get here soon, Dragos. Or your baby mama is going to give birth in prison.

"Are you sure?" Carling asked.

"It's okay." She could hear the lie in her own voice, and she was certain that the other woman could too. The last thing she wanted to do was to offer her wrist up to the nightmarish creature crouching beside her. Gritting her teeth, she stuck out her arm. "Really. Here."

Carling's red gaze held hers as she took hold of Pia's arm. Pia had more than enough time to regret her offer. Carling was severely undernourished. What if she couldn't stop drinking once she had started?

Then the Vampyre lowered her head. With a flash of white fangs, she bit into the soft flesh at Pia's inner wrist and drank. When she finished, she licked the puncture wounds to seal them, thanked Pia, and eased away. She didn't look any better—she had lost far too much blood to be adequately nourished by the small amount she had taken from Pia—but at least she did seem to move more easily.

There was nothing left to do. Pia drank more water, curled on her side, and tried to nap, but the cave floor was too hard, and she was too anxious to relax. As soon as the sunshine had shifted away and the outside ledge lay in shadow, Carling edged over to the opening. Using the arrow, she began to scrape at the fresh concrete base at the bar in the farthest corner. Neither woman spoke.

Pia's first contractions started just as the sun went down.

Chapter Six

THE WAIT TO hear from the kidnappers was excruciating.

The part of Dragos's mind that was so good at statistics kept running calculations on the odds of Pia's and Carling's survival. As time passed, that calculation turned grim.

The person who had texted with him clearly had a sadistic bent. Most kidnappers would have been eager to get to the point. They would have made their demands known by now, because the longer they kept their hostages, the greater their risk of discovery.

No, this person wanted to hurt him. That did not bode well for how they would be treating the women.

As Dragos and the rest of the wedding party combed the city for clues throughout the night, they coalesced into a coherent team. Every casino in Las Vegas agreed to lift their magic dampeners and close their gambling floors. The police assigned a liaison to work with Dragos and the others.

Word of Eva's condition came back from the hospital. She had needed surgery and was being kept in an induced coma until the swelling in her brain went down, but the doctors were confident she would make a full recovery over time. It was one bright spot in the grim, black night.

The Light Fae Queen, Tatiana, opened the Riverview Casino's resources to them, and they set up operations in the casino's conference rooms.

"I do not forget how your sentinel Graydon helped when my daughter was kidnapped," she told Dragos in a quick phone call. "I also remember the assistance you and Pia gave us when we were attacked by my sister Isabeau. If there is anything more the Light Fae demesne can do for you, don't hesitate to ask."

It was a significant offer. That fact managed to worm its way through the savagery winding like a serpent around Dragos's heart.

Even the owners of the Bellagio were less than apoplectic at the damage done to their property. Instead, they approached the issue in a businesslike manner and engaged a team of insurance assessors without delay.

Local and national news outlets picked up the film clips of Dragos's impulsive offer of rewards, and the Wyr crime hotline number was inundated with hundreds of phone calls. That number would soon be in the thousands. The great majority of the calls were useless, but every one that seemed like it could be substantive needed to be verified.

Politicians still condemned the cavalier destruction of public property, but they also expressed their deepest sympathy for the difficulty of the Wyr lord's situation.

As far as the investigation went, several people were arrested and detained for questioning. Fifteen workers at the Bellagio had been bribed by an unknown party to report details on the wedding party's activities and whereabouts, which was no doubt why the resort owners were so subdued at the damage Dragos had caused.

And as the night bled away into another fierce desert day, they analyzed the security footage from the Riverview frame by frame.

Dragos and Rune watched the footage of Pia's kidnapping obsessively. There was no security footage on how Carling had been taken. With facial recognition software, they were able to manipulate individual frames to get partial snapshots of the kidnappers' faces. They saw something that looked like it might be a logo on a few members of the team, but when they tried to blow the images up, it blurred too much to be legible.

They had several shots of the Elven woman, who was clearly the leader, but the scar across her face prevented the software from analyzing her features enough to get any hits from criminal databases. Either that or she had managed to avoid being caught and catalogued up until now.

That woman. Dragos traced her face with one of his talons that refused to retract. That woman was the most familiar scent from the rooftop. He could feel it in his bones.

Rune was as grim and closed down as Dragos, but

aside from the strain of the situation, it was remarkable how easily they fell back into a working relationship.

At one point Dragos stopped what he was doing to look at the other man. "I have missed you."

Rune's gaze flared up to meet his. The expression in his eyes was raw. After a moment, he gave a short nod. "Too bad it had to be like this."

Dragos put his hand on the other man's shoulder, pressing with his fingers. Too bad, indeed.

When a text came, both of their phones pinged at once. Snatching up his phone, Dragos opened the message and stared at a photo of Pia and a skeletal Vampyre, both unconscious in what looked to be a cave that had been converted into a cell.

The text came next. I wonder how things are going to go when the cellmates wake up?

Rage and terror roared. Pia was trapped with a Vampyre who had been so drained she didn't look human any longer.

Rune's face clenched. He whispered, "Goddamn them to hell."

Dragos growled, unable to speak. The need for violence flashed through his body. When Rune looked up, his expression changed.

Advancing on Dragos, he snapped, "She wouldn't! Dragos, she won't. No—don't lose control!"

His words didn't penetrate. Dragos looked around the large conference room that was strewn with computers, phones, files, and untouched food in take-out containers. It all looked alien and offensive to his animal nature. His body heated so that his clothes began to smoke. All he could think of was setting everything on fire.

A hard blow hit him in the chest, knocking him back several feet. Even as he recovered his balance, Rune hit him again with the flat of his hand. The gryphon's expression was hard, his jaw iron tight.

"You listen to me," he growled. "Carling would die before she laid a finger on Pia and the baby."

Dragos shoved Rune's hand away. "The blood thirst," he snapped. "They've pushed her to the edge of her resources."

"Don't you think I can see what they've done to her? *I know!*" Rune roared. Tears sprang to his eyes. He got in Dragos's face. "You've always had a prejudice against Carling! She's too cunning and manipulative for you— because she's just like you. Well, somehow we all found a way to love you anyway, you asshole, and you know why? Because we see something in you that is worth it, and it's the same for Carling. I've staked my life on it. I know that woman inside and out. And she will. Not. Hurt. Pia. So get a grip. We've got to figure out how we're going to respond."

Gradually Dragos calmed enough for Rune's angry words to penetrate. "You're right," he said, very low. "I've not been fair to Carling."

"Damn right," Rune snapped. The gryphon looked down at his phone, clenched in one hand. Angrily he swiped the tears from his face. "They are so fucking dead for this. I'm going to slaughter every one of them."

Dragos became aware that almost everyone had left the conference room except for Aryal, Graydon, and Bayne, who had watched the confrontation with sober attentiveness. With their mates taken, Rune and Dragos were not safe to be around, and the sentinels were watching them for signs of danger.

Dragos forwarded the photo to them. "See if Grace or anybody else can get some kind of psychic hit off this. Find out if Khalil can transport to this place."

"Wouldn't that be fucking amazing if the Djinn could drop us all in the middle of that scene?" Bayne said. "I'm on it."

As the big sentinel strode out, Dragos turned back to Rune. "If we provoke them, they might do worse to the women."

"Agreed," Rune gritted.

Dragos texted, Are you ready to talk terms?

No reply. What could he say or do to break the icy impasse on the other end?

You're a murderous monstrosity that should have been hunted down and exterminated centuries ago.

This whole thing was about him. Not Rune, not Carling, not Pia. Rune hadn't even gotten a message from the kidnappers until now.

He typed, I'm the one you want. Let the women go and take me instead. We can arrange a trade.

The reply came back quickly. `We're almost ready for you. Wait for my word.`

Wait for your word? Dragos thought. A feral smile stretched his lips across hard teeth. Like hell I will.

Finally he understood why Azrael had come to Las Vegas. He hadn't welcomed Death's presence before, but he did now.

The dragon turned his attention back to the hunt.

Bayne reported back. Khalil very much regretted he could not transport to the place in the photo. Something about the scene blocked his magic.

Grace had much the same problem, but her message was more cryptic, and she came to deliver it in person. She was a pretty young woman with titian hair and a permanent limp from an old injury, and her lover Khalil stood protectively by her side.

"This may not be useful," the young Oracle said. "So I don't want take too much of your time, but there's something about us that isn't in focus."

On the other side of the conference table, Dragos paced as he listened. "What do you mean?"

"I'm trying to put it into words." She looked frustrated and gestured at the whiteboard on one wall. "They are over there—wherever there is—and we can't see them properly."

Rune bit out, "That's not news."

"I know." She gave him a compassionate glance. "Bear with me. I think the concept is important. All we have to do to see them better is… adjust our lens. It's not just that they're hidden. That's on their side of things. I'm talking about our side of things."

Dragos frowned. "We are not doing something that we could be doing to see them better."

"Exactly," the Oracle said. "There is something we are not seeing that we could be seeing. I keep getting a camera image—changing the focus. Changing how we see the focus. Maybe even changing who sees the focus. The point is, we either have information or an image of something that we are not seeing properly."

Dragos looked at Rune. "That's a big difference from not having information."

"Yeah, okay." Rune ran his fingers through his hair. "But what are we not seeing?"

Dragos looked at Grace. "You said three things. Changing the focus, changing how we see the focus, and changing who sees the focus. And it's all about the camera."

She blew out a frustrated sigh and lifted her hands. "That's all I've got. I'm sorry, I wish it was more."

"Has everybody in the wedding party seen the video footage we have of the kidnappers?" he asked. Graydon's mate Beluviel, who was also quite pregnant, was an elder from the Elven demesne in South Carolina and had once been one of the leaders. While there were Elven communities all over the world, and it was unrealistic to hope Bel could know all of them, the scar across the Elven woman's face was distinctive, and it was worth a shot. "Collectively we all hold a great deal of information. Call everyone together. Have them go through the still photos and watch the footage."

It took almost an hour for all thirteen members of the wedding party to leave their various tasks and converge on the conference room, including Dr. Medina. Bel had been at the hospital, monitoring Eva's progress, and she was one of the last to arrive.

It was all Dragos could do to keep from snatching her up and physically plopping her into a seat. As soon as Bel stepped inside, he said, "Play the footage and pass the photos around."

This is probably a waste of time, Rune muttered telepathically.

He shot a glare at the gryphon. *We've got nothing else to try.*

He watched Bel intently. When the footage reached the part where one of the kidnappers slammed the butt of the gun into the back of Eva's head, the beautiful woman winced. "Concentrate," he said to her. "Do you recognize that Elf?"

"I'm sorry, I don't. Do you mind if I send one of the photos of her around to some people? Maybe to my stepson, Ferion?"

Ferion was now Lord of the Elven demesne in South Carolina, and while Dragos would never be liked by the Elves, Pia was quite popular with them. They would care about her well-being.

Dragos told Bel, "Please do—but only to those whose discretion you can rely upon. If we go too public with these photos, we might goad them into treating Pia and Carling with more cruelty."

"I understand." She gave him a sober look.

As she took pictures of several photos with her cell phone, he turned to the others. "The rest of you—do you see anything?"

"We're going to watch it again," Rune said.

No one complained. Every one of them pored over the footage and the photos, Grace too. Dragos sent all the Wyr up to the rooftop to see if any of them got a hit off the scents. As the day plummeted to evening, he summoned Dr. Medina over.

"She had emergency syringes with her, but her purse isn't with her in the photo," he said in a low voice.

Medina didn't sugarcoat anything, which was something that Dragos normally liked about her. She told him, "I'll assemble an emergency medical team to be on standby. If you have ever been inclined to bargain with a Djinn, now would be the time to do so."

He closed his eyes. There seemed to be no limit to the depths of this plunge. "Understood. Khalil?"

Instantly, the Djinn left Grace's side and crossed the room. "Yes?"

"We need another Djinn. Your help is invaluable, but we need someone who will stay exclusively with Medina and her medical team."

Khalil's physical form was that of a tall, imperious-looking man with long raven hair and the signature piercing, diamond-like eyes of the Djinn. He frowned.

"My daughter is away. I will find someone suitable."

"Tell them the Lord of the Wyr will owe them a favor," Dragos said.

"No," Grace said as she joined them. "I have so many Djinn who owe me favors, I will never be able to use them all in one lifetime. Let me do this for you."

"Thank you," Dragos told her. "I won't forget it." Raising his voice, he spoke to everyone in the room. "I won't forget how all of you have helped."

Sometime later, as he stood at one of the large picture windows watching the sunset, Beluviel stood so quickly her chair toppled over behind her. Dragos spun around.

Waving her phone in the air, she said loudly, "I've got it! I've got her name! A member of Ferion's council recognized her. It's Caerlovena!"

Duncan and Seremela looked at each other, their expressions flaring with excitement. Duncan said, "We know that name, although we never met her. She was in Devil's Gate when we were there."

"Where's Devil's Gate?" Rune leaped at a computer console and began typing.

"It's in northwest Nevada. There's a kind of modern-day gold rush going on out there—only what people are looking for is magic-sensitive silver. We negotiated with Malphas there and got Seremela's niece out of some serious trouble."

In another part of the room, Luis rubbed his mouth and said, "That 'gold rush' has been going on ever since

Claudia and I uncovered the slave ring where they were mining in Nirvana. I heard they've been building an actual town in Devil's Gate."

Dragos had heard of it too. He always paid attention to anything involving precious metals and jewels. But at the moment none of that mattered. The only thing that did matter was the *snick* he felt as the information came together. Now he understood what Grace meant by coming into focus.

Rune said with fierce triumph, "I've got latitude and longitude coordinates."

"*Caerlovena*," the dragon breathed. Smoke poured out of his mouth and swirled around the conference-room floor.

In that moment there was nothing sweeter than the taste of his prey's name on his lips.

Chapter Seven

THE CONSTANT *SCRAPE scrape scrape* of the arrow against the concrete was driving Pia bonkers, but she didn't complain because it looked like Carling might actually be making some progress.

The Vampyre kept brushing bits of debris into a careful pile with one skeletal hand. It seemed she had some use for it, and as the sun set, she appeared to gain some strength and energy.

Pia breathed through the contractions and tried to time them as she watched Carling work. It was impossible to get any kind of accurate time without a watch, of course, but she counted up the rhythmic scrapes and did her best to estimate.

Maybe she was having Braxton–Hicks contractions. The past couple of days had certainly been stressful enough. She might not be going into real labor yet.

She held on to that hope until the baby gave a gigantic kick. Suddenly she had to go to the bathroom urgently, and she struggled to her feet to rush over to the bucket. Just as she squatted, a deluge of liquid gushed out.

Carling spun around, focusing on her with laser-like intensity. "Your water broke, didn't it?" the Vampyre said. "I can smell blood."

Near to tears, Pia nodded as she tried to readjust her clothes. She'd gotten lucky. Most of the liquid had ended up in the bucket, but she was still damp in places. "I guess I've been in labor for a couple of hours."

As she straightened, the cave spun around her. Carling sprang to her side and grabbed her by the elbows.

Helping her to ease down to the ground again, Carling exclaimed, "Why didn't you say anything?"

"There wasn't anything anybody could do." Pia curled on her side. "I kept hoping they were Braxton–Hicks." She had grown a little easier around the Vampyre's feral red gaze, but not by much.

Carling said, "Maybe if I can get someone's attention, they'll give us some supplies. Towels, fresh water. Hot water if we can talk them into it."

As Carling started to stand, Pia lunged upward to grab her arm. "No, don't! The last time I came to Caerlovena's attention, she shot at me. The only reason the baby and I are still alive is because we got lucky. What if you hadn't been able to catch the arrow in time? What if next time she brings a gun and empties a clip at us?"

Carling looked around the wretched cave. Aside from a little water left in the plastic jug, they had nothing. Watching the Vampyre grind her teeth was a macabre experience.

"Fine," she said. "I understand. I'm going to make some cloth strips. We'll need something to swaddle the baby with, and hopefully we'll have enough to give you a pad afterward."

"Neither one of us is wearing shorts—yet. And I've got a bra. I can lose my top without having to go bare naked." Pia pushed herself upright again and pulled off her tunic.

"I don't need my top either, and I don't have a modern sense of modesty. I don't have any problem going nude if the situation warrants it. How far apart are your contractions?"

"I don't know. Not too far." She rubbed her face with a shaking hand.

Carling said in steady voice, "We're going to get through this, Pia. Women give birth all the time during war. They give birth in farm fields and ditches. I've attended many births before, and I know what to do. I understand this isn't what anybody would have wanted for you, but it's going to be okay."

"Got it." Carling's words did help. A contraction was coming. Pia gritted her teeth. "If they can do it, I can do it. I've survived Dragos's bout of amnesia and a zombie apocalypse. I can give birth to Stinkpot in a cave if I have to."

"That's my girl." Using her sharp white fangs, Carling tore her own top into strips, then started on Pia's. "We need to swaddle the baby and have enough afterward to strap him to your torso. I want you able to get on your feet and run if we get the chance."

A snort escaped Pia as she looked at the bars. "You're going to have to do a lot of digging to get my fat ass out of here. I think I might be a three-bar heist."

The Vampyre gave a ghost of a chuckle. "The shape I'm in right now, I'm probably a one-bar heist, especially if I can bend the neighboring bar a little. All I need to do is make sure I have enough space to get my head through. If I can do that, I can wiggle out."

Pia realized she had gone from being afraid of Carling to being grateful for the other woman's presence. Giving birth was not clean or dignified. Soon she was going to be at the mercy of her own body, and the conditions they were in were appalling, but somehow Carling's steady pragmatism turned the whole nightmare into something that was somewhat bearable.

Then a remarkably disgusting thought occurred to her, but she set her teeth against the urge to gag. Carling was starving. They didn't have room for niceties. She met the other woman's gaze. "There'll be a lot of blood in the afterbirth."

"Yes, there will." The Vampyre smiled in approval.

"If you manage to dislodge one of those bars, you need to go ahead without me," Pia told her. "Don't stay here, not if you can get out. You could feed and regain some of your strength. You might be able get hold of a cell phone."

"Also, if I can get away from these magic-dampening

bars, I could cast spells." Carling rolled the strips into rolls. "All very good points. I need to get back to digging. Rest when you can, walk around if it helps, and let me know when the contractions are very close together or when you can't control the urge to push."

"Okay."

She watched Carling get back to work.

Inside the cave, the shadows were deepening. Outside looked a bit lighter, closer to dusk than full night. She had gotten used to the background noise of people hammering and working. At one point they brought a crane in to lift the top part of the dragon into place. Its wooden head was almost at the level of the cave entrance.

When the activity had stopped, it had seemed too quiet, but respite from noise was brief.

Soon came a different sound, the buzz of many voices coming together. Suddenly Carling scraped her pile of debris into the growing hole she had created at the base of the bar she'd been working on. She moved away quickly.

The reason why became clear soon enough. Caerlovena walked onto the ledge in front of the cave, carrying a megaphone. She wore light armor and was armed with a gun holstered at her hip and a sword strapped between her broad shoulders. Her back was to the cave, and she faced out to the clearing. Two attendants flanked her, each one carrying a lamp.

Unable to stand the vulnerability of being on the

ground with Caerlovena so near, Pia pushed to her feet. As she did, she noticed how Carling had changed. Instead of looking like the rather friendly nightmare she had almost gotten used to, the Vampyre gripped her arrow like a spear, her body taut as a bow.

Did she mean to *throw* the arrow at Caerlovena?

Stepping in front of Carling, Pia went face-to-face with her. "Don't," she whispered. "We need that arrow."

The Vampyre breathed, "If I were at full strength, I could do it."

"You're not at full strength." Pia stared her down. "And even if you could, maybe you could accept the consequences, but I couldn't. The only person you would kill is Caerlovena, and there are a lot of other people out there. I need my baby to get out of this alive."

The tension drained slowly from Carling's emaciated body. "You're right, of course."

As Pia sagged with relief, Caerlovena lifted the megaphone and spoke. "People of Devil's Gate, welcome to the lighting of the dragon's pyre! Each one of you is important. You are all here for a purpose. By your presence tonight you are making a covenant—you agree with me that the dragon has to die. He has been a blight upon this earth for far too long. I've captured his pregnant mate, and now he has no other choice but to respond. Prepare yourselves, and make no mistake about it, we are going to war!"

As the Elven woman spoke, Pia and Carling edged over to the bars to look out over the clearing. Pia's heart sank at the sight of just how many people had gathered in a huge circle around the dragon effigy.

There had to be thousands present—Elves, Vampyres and other Nightkind, trolls, ghouls, Demonkind, and humans.

She whispered, "I had no idea he was hated by so many people."

Carling put a bracing hand at her back. "Don't let this ridiculous piece of theater fool you. Caerlovena isn't leading a community. She's running a cult. The majority of these are Elves, and all of them are crazy. Dragos has his fair share of supporters too. Besides, these bars are messing with my magic sense, but I think she has some sort of charismatic magic."

While they spoke, Caerlovena stalked back and forth along the length of the ledge, whipping her supporters into a frenzy. With every declaration she made, the crowd roared in approval.

Even Pia had to reluctantly admit she was a chilling, magnificent sight. Whether Caerlovena was casting actual magic or not, she definitely had some spell over the crowd. They loved her.

"And now—set him on fire!" Caerlovena shouted. "*Watch him burn!*"

Down below, several Elves ran forward carrying lit torches and touched them to the stacks of wood. They must have treated the woodpile with some sort of accelerant, because the fire caught quickly and grew in strength as it spread over the base. Hungry flames began to leap up the dragon effigy.

Good gods, someone in the crowd even had drums. A thrumming tribal rhythm filled the clearing, and the crowd below began to dance with wild abandon. Caerlovena laughed as she watched them. The whole thing was like something out of a 1970s James Bond movie.

As Pia watched the remarkable scene in equal parts fascination and horror, a vise gripped her around the middle. Clinging to the bars, she panted through the contraction. It was hard to imagine how things could get any worse.

Until, that was, a tall black-haired man in a dark suit walked into the clear space surrounding the burning effigy. He had green eyes and wore a more classically handsome version of Dragos's features.

Death had come to join the gathering.

Pia started to shake. Nudging Carling, she whispered, "Look down below, in the clear space near the effigy. Do you see that man?"

The Vampyre ran her gaze over the clearing. "See who? That fire's too big and too hot for anyone to get very close."

Azrael looked up in the direction of the cave. Perhaps it was a trick of the growing firelight, but it seemed as though he looked directly at Pia.

She had been wrong. Things were about to get much worse.

The flames reached the top of the effigy. It threw off

so much heat Pia could feel it where she stood, and as true night set in, the red light illuminated the clearing and everything around it.

Her thigh started to itch maddeningly. Then the itch traveled up her right shoulder and arm. As she scratched herself, she could feel large patches of raised bumps on her skin. She had broken out in hives. Soon after that, nausea churned. Without the drug protocol to keep her body in check, it was beginning to rebel in style.

Abruptly, she hurried over to the bucket to throw up. Once she had cleared her stomach of all its contents, she felt marginally better. As she wiped her mouth with the back of one hand, she realized Carling had joined her and was holding back her hair.

The Vampyre said softly, "You're not doing so well, are you, honey?"

"My body is rejecting the baby while I am also giving birth," Pia told her in a flat, matter-of-fact voice. The specter of this scenario, or another one like it, had been hanging over her head for the entire pregnancy. "Now that it's started, the only way out of this is by going through it."

When she was finally able to straighten, Carling handed her the plastic jug of water. She took a few swallows, one to rinse out her mouth and spit and another to ease the rawness of her abused throat.

Capping the jug, she turned toward the cave opening just as a gigantic bronze meteor plummeted to earth. It landed on the burning effigy, which exploded into flaming missiles that shot out over the clearing.

Dragos had arrived.

Roaring, the dragon spun, shockingly fast for a creature of his size, and he spewed flames in a wide circle around him. Overhead a harpy screamed and swooped. She was joined by three magnificent gryphons, each one easily the size of an SUV. The crowd plunged and shrieked as burning pieces of wood rained down.

Pia stared, transfixed. The scene was so overwhelmingly cataclysmic, for a moment it transported her out of her misery.

"Stop! Stop!" Caerlovena bellowed into her megaphone. Pulling her gun, she aimed at Pia. *"Dragon, if you don't stop right now, I will shoot her!"*

Time held still. Pia stopped breathing as she stared from the barrel of the gun to Dragos, then back again. Was he too far gone in his frenzy to hear Caerlovena?

Deliberately Carling stepped in front of her, but the Vampyre's emaciated body could not stop a hail of bullets, especially if she took a fatal shot herself and collapsed into dust.

Fixing his immense gold gaze on Caerlovena, the dragon stopped.

A sound echoed over the clearing. It sounded bizarre under the circumstances. Caerlovena was laughing.

The Elven woman said to the dragon, "You're here a little ahead of schedule, but that's nothing we can't work with. Send your people away—all of them except for the Vampyre's mate. I want them far away, on the other side of my forest's border."

Dragos lifted his head to the other Wyr and growled, "Go."

One by one the others lifted into the air and flew away. The harpy left shrieking in rage while Rune slammed to the ground beside Dragos. The gryphon looked as wild and feral as Pia felt as he stared up at the cliff at his mate.

With the two Wyr held immobile, the milling chaos around the clearing gradually stopped.

"That's it, now we're talking," Caerlovena said. Triumph caused her voice to go shrill. "Now… Change back into your human forms."

The air shimmered around them, and both dragon and gryphon disappeared, to be replaced by two men standing side by side. They were both dressed in a similar fashion, in jeans, T-shirt, and boots, with swords strapped to their backs and guns holstered at their hips, but that was where the similarity ended.

Physically they looked very different. Rune stood over six feet tall and had the graceful build of a swordsman, handsome good looks, and golden hair, while Dragos was taller, rougher, and his hair was black like a raven's wing. Clusters of burning firewood surrounded them. The only other figure for yards around was Azrael, who stood like an immobile statue looking out over the scene.

Rune didn't appear to notice Death, but Pia noticed that Dragos did. He gave Azrael a long look before turning his attention back up to the cave. His hard face was expressionless, but his eyes burned hot gold. He might be cloaked in his human form, but he had still completely given himself over to the dragon.

"See how easily the Great Beast can be controlled!" Caerlovena screamed.

Lady, if you think he's controlled you are delusional, Pia thought as she stared down at Dragos. This is the calm before the cyclone hits. Right now he's just biding his time.

But there was something about Caerlovena that Pia was finally beginning to understand. The Elven woman really didn't care about the consequences of her actions. She wasn't like some cartoonish 1970s James Bond villain, swollen with her own importance and invincibility. She probably already knew she wasn't going to survive this encounter. Too many people knew what she had done.

The only thing she cared about was killing Dragos, and that reckless disregard of self carried its own kind of danger. It left her capable of doing anything.

As Caerlovena roared into her megaphone and whipped her followers back into a frenzy, another contraction hit. Pia hunched over, panting until it passed. When she straightened again, the expressionlessness had vanished from Dragos's features.

Staring at her fiercely, he mouthed, "Do your job. Stay alive."

Swiping at her damp face with the back of one hand,

she nodded and mouthed back, "Do your job. Get us out of here."

He gave her a slight nod in reply.

It was a miserably meager exchange. She wanted to lean back against his chest like she had when she had given birth to Liam. She wanted his arms around her, his voice in her ear as he coached her through each contraction. Hell, she wanted Dr. Medina and a private room at the nearest hospital.

None of that was going to happen.

"Good thing I already know you're a firecracker," she whispered to the baby as she rubbed her belly soothingly. "Looks like it's you and me, kiddo."

"And me."

That interjection had not come from Carling. The Vampyre was still standing taut at the bars, watching Rune.

Slowly Pia turned, eyes wide and staring. Azrael stood beside her.

As she backed away, she said hoarsely, "You get away from me. Neither one of us is dying."

He followed. When she came back against the cave wall, he leaned one broad shoulder against the wall beside her. "People always take it so personally when I arrive. They act like I'm out to get them," Azrael remarked. "I applaud your will to live. It may see you through this."

"Do something useful. Get me some hot water and towels."

"My role is not to interfere with the living," he told her. "But I can ease your death if it comes to that."

"Are you physically here?" She panted. As rage flared, she slapped him.

His head rocked back, and his gaze flared in surprise.

Her hand hurt. She shook it out. She'd had too many choices taken away from her. Slapping someone felt good, and she wanted to do it again.

"Don't stand here in the physical world and tell me you can't physically do something," she hissed. "That's bullshit. Oh, woo-woo, you might be Death, but big fucking deal. Death is as common as dirt. Dragos *lives* in the physical world. He takes action—he's immersed in it. You're just using your elevated social status to keep a barrier between you and everybody else!"

"Dragos does what is in his nature, as do we all," Azrael bit out. His previous detachment had disappeared. Now he looked furious.

"Well, your nature sucks, asshole," she snarled. "If you're going to be useless, get out of my way. I've got a baby to deliver."

Releasing an angry breath, he turned to her and reached for her swollen stomach. As she shrank back, he said impatiently, "Do you really think I have to touch you for your baby to die—or that I want to kill him? Like I said, *everybody* thinks I'm out to get them. You said you wanted help, so hold still! I'm not going to hurt you."

Shaking, breathing hard, she managed not to totally

lose it as she watched him touch her stomach. His hand was warm, not icy cold as she had feared.

Numbness spread outward from his touch. More than a little freaked out, she pinched herself. She felt it. It was not so much numbness, then, as a lack of pain. When the next contraction came, she felt it as a tightening of her muscles.

"Okay," she said grudgingly. "That's not nothing, I guess, so thank you. Although if you really wanted to be helpful, you'd get me some fucking towels and hot water. After all, I'm pretty sure they won't do anything drastic like unnaturally prolong my life."

"You would be surprised," he said, arching one eyebrow. "One small change can create large differences over time. In case you haven't heard of it before, it's called the butterfly effect."

She rolled her eyes. "I guess I'll have to understand if the possibility of creating change is too much for you to handle. No doubt you can't sully your reputation by acting like someone who gives a shit."

Azrael regarded her, his mouth tight. "You're quite something when you get going, you know that?"

"Oh please," she said. "Tell it to someone who cares."

As before at the Midnight Lounge, neither Carling nor Caerlovena and her two attendants appeared to notice Azrael's presence in the cave. Their focus was on the clearing below.

"Just like the Lord of the Wyr and his sentinel

games, we are going to have our own tournament," Caerlovena said with a savage smile. "Line up, patriots, and ready yourselves for battle. Only, unlike the dragon's grandstanding, we're not going to fight one-on-one. No, we're going to fight Dragos and his pet gryphon all together." She pointed at the two men. "And you will remain in your human forms. You'll refrain from casting magic during the battle, or I'll have my men empty their guns into this cave until there's nothing left alive. Is that clear?"

"Crystal," Dragos snapped. He and Rune pulled their swords and turned so that they stood back-to-back while the crowd gathered in a tight circle around them.

Nonstop dread had become Pia's new normal. She said to Azrael, "If Dragos is like you, he can't die, can he?"

"Everyone can die," Azrael replied. "Even those of us you call the Primal Powers can die. If Dragos dies, another Great Beast will simply rise to take his place."

Another beast—like Liam?

No. Just *no.*

"That's not what I wanted to hear," she muttered.

But Azrael was no longer there. He had pulled his favorite disappearing trick and had left the cave.

She tightened her hand into a fist. Good thing her slapping hand was still throbbing, otherwise she might believe she had hallucinated the whole thing.

But once that thought had occurred, she couldn't shake it.

The only thing she really knew for sure was that she had hit something with her slapping hand. Then the *what-ifs* started to cascade.

What if she had been hallucinating all along? What if she had slapped the cave wall?

What if her growing numbness wasn't a gift from Death?

What if it was a warning sign instead?

Chapter Eight

CAERLOVENA'S ARMY RUSHED toward Dragos and Rune.

"Here we go," Rune muttered. "Got any bright ideas?"

"You mean aside from slaughtering everyone?" Dragos retorted. He would be quite fine with that plan, except if and when their enemies thinned down too significantly, he knew Caerlovena would start shooting into the cave anyway, just to ensure nobody survived. "I'm working on it."

Death walked along the open area between the attackers and the two men, hands in his pockets. Azrael looked contemplative, lips pursed in thought, until Dragos lost sight of him as the first wave of attackers hit.

Then he got on with the business of killing.

Rune spun, dashed, and leaped his way through the crowd. Fighters fell wherever he passed. The gryphon was perfection in motion, fast and graceful as a dancer yet powerful enough to hammer down with his massive strength when the situation warranted it.

Catching glimpses of the other male in full warrior

mode reminded Dragos of why he had picked Rune to be his First sentinel all those many years ago.

Okay fine, he said telepathically to Rune. *Maybe Carling isn't so bad after all.*

Giving him a filthy look, Rune just barely managed to avoid getting his skull caved in by a troll wielding a war hammer. *You pick NOW as your time to get talkative? Man, I have all the sympathetic feelings for Pia.*

Taking a running leap, Dragos landed on the troll's back and stabbed his sword into the crevice between the troll's rocklike skull and neck. Trumpeting a noise that sounded like a wounded elk, the troll staggered. It was already dead, but it would take a few moments to fall.

He didn't wait around but jumped off and grabbed the troll's war hammer. After hefting it in approval, he whirled and flung it hard at another troll some fifteen paces away. It smashed into the second troll's face, and when that one fell, it took out another five warriors who were standing too close to it.

Maximum damage. He liked that. He needed to do more of it.

If he could only cut loose with all his abilities, he would show that Elven bitch some maximum damage. There would be nothing left in this clearing except some blackened bones. That was what had happened to her war party, millennia ago.

As soon as he had laid eyes on her in person and heard her speak, he had remembered her. She was not part of the past he had lost when he had sustained his head injury. She was from well before that time, back in the ancient days before humans had begun to walk the earth.

Caerlovena and her war party had come to slay the dragon. That had not gone well for any of them. In fact, the scar she bore to this day was from that ancient battle with Dragos. Healing spells were not very effective in treating wounds caused by dragon fire.

She had attacked *him* and then had carried a sense of grievance all these years because things hadn't gone her way. *Goddamn Elves.*

Now she held all four of them in a tight trap. He and Rune could cover each other's backs on the field well enough, because even though there were thousands against the two of them, the physical limitations of hand-to-hand fighting meant they faced maybe seven to ten warriors at any given time—and none of them were a match for the two Wyr.

The problem was, the longer the battle lasted, the more damage they sustained. Rune already carried several cuts and bruises, as did Dragos. If the two of them didn't employ any of their other abilities, Caerlovena's army would gradually win by wearing them down through sheer force of numbers.

Meanwhile, Pia was in labor. She and the baby needed to be in the hospital with Wyr healers. Carling needed medical attention too, but in Dragos's opinion Pia was the real urgent situation.

As he fought, he kept an eye on Caerlovena and her

two attendants stationed at the cave entrance. Caerlovena paced back and forth, shouting raucous encouragement to her fighters in the clearing until Dragos wanted to ram that fucking megaphone down her throat.

"Oh, we're having fun now, aren't we?" she shouted.

And really, as Dragos looked at the growing pile of dead bodies that surrounded him and Rune, that last bit was too much.

"I don't know, Caerlovena," he shouted back. "It looks to me like you're too fucking cowardly to come down here and fight yourself. All you've done so far is kidnap and threaten a pregnant woman, stand out of harm's way, and get everybody else to do your dirty work for you!"

The intensity of the fighting around them eased as some of Caerlovena's fighters pulled back, doubt flashing across their faces.

Caerlovena glared at Dragos, her powerful body tense with rage. "You seem to think you're owed a fair fight, dragon. Nothing could be further from the truth! Did any of my people get a fair fight?"

"Your people came to attack me," he snarled. Smoking blood dripped down his arm from a cut. He carried so much pent-up rage in his body his blood hissed with it. He swung his arm, flinging the blood at his nearest opponents. They screamed and stumbled back as it sprayed their faces.

"Because you hunted us first!" she screamed.

"Somebody had to kill you!"

"My point remains—you're too cowardly to come down here and fight me yourself!" He injected enough force into his words to project to everyone in the clearing as he gestured to the piles of bodies strewn around them. "Instead, you're sending all of them to their deaths."

If looks could kill, her gaze would be shooting a spear through his chest. "Pull back," she said into megaphone. "Everybody, pull back!"

Her followers obeyed, eyeing Rune and Dragos warily as they retreated until they stood at the edge of the clearing.

Caerlovena waited until her army stood quiet and attentive. Then she said in a calm, cold voice, "My point remains as well. You seem to think you're owed a fair fight. That's not what this is—this is only round one. Let me tell you what round two is, dragon. You and your gryphon are going to fight each other to the death."

"No," he said flatly.

She gave him a vicious smile. "Yes. If you don't fight, I will kill both your mates right now. If you do fight, only one of you has to die."

Dragos growled, "Caerlovena, we both heard that lie. You have no intention of letting either one of us live."

Her smile widened. "What real choice do you have, and how far will you go for a few more minutes of life?"

He exchanged a grim glance with Rune. Sweat darkened the gryphon's hair, and his T-shirt was soaked in blood. When Dragos glanced up at the mouth of the cave, both Carling and Pia had disappeared. His gut tightened. The only reason why they would have walked away from this confrontation was because something else more urgent demanded their attention.

One of her attendants nudged her shoulder. Dragos could hear him perfectly as he whispered, "My lady— *look*."

As she turned to stare into the cave, Dragos caught a whiff of Pia's blood on the breeze. Despite the carnage that surrounded him and Rune, he would know her scent anywhere, anytime. Raw fear slashed at him with razored claws.

"Who did that?" Caerlovena exclaimed. Then, in a louder, enraged shout, "Who did that? *How did that get in there? HOW DID SOMEBODY GET INTO THIS CAVE?*"

Her other attendant turned to stare into the cave as well.

For one pulse beat, none of three people standing on the ledge paid any attention to what happened in the clearing below.

Dragos lunged.

Pushing harder than he had ever pushed in his life, he raced at the cliff face. As he ran, he cast a panic spell that blasted out from him like an atomic bomb. When the wave hit the surrounding army, they plunged into screaming chaos.

In the same moment he *leaped*, arms outstretched. No time to leap, cast magic, and shapeshift all at once.

Instead, he strained upward, reaching, reaching—and he achieved just enough height to grab hold of Caerlovena's ankle in one hand, and the ankle of one of her attendants in the other.

As he did so, a gryphon shot past overhead, arrowing in murderous silence toward the second attendant. On the same intolerable hair trigger as Dragos, Rune had acted the very moment he had.

Caerlovena and the attendant Dragos had grabbed lurched as he yanked them off-balance. With an enraged scream, she drew her gun and spun to face him. He braced one foot against the face of the cliff and shoved hard.

As he fell backward, he dragged both his prey down with him.

Even as they fell, Caerlovena brought the muzzle of her gun up. Bullets tore into Dragos's body. He didn't know how many. He wasn't counting; he didn't care. All he cared about was her expression of terrified horror.

All three slammed onto the ground together. Pushing to move despite a wave of searing pain, Dragos flipped to land on top of the Elven woman's body.

Ah, splendid. She wasn't dead yet. He knocked her gun away and got her into a headlock. Struggling against his weight, she coughed and reached back to claw at him, trying to gouge out his eyes.

Turning his face from her clawing fingers, he tightened his hold around her neck. Civilized thought had vaporized, obliterated by the dragon's rage. Only one rule of law remained, the oldest and most savage in the Great Beast's domain—kill or be killed.

He had her. He had her, and he could have made her ending quick.

"You're a cruel coward," he whispered in her ear. Her body strained and arched as she fought to breathe, and his hot blood soaked into the clothes on her back. "Only a true monster would treat a pregnant woman the way you did. You don't deserve a quick death."

She couldn't talk any longer, but she could telepathize. *I'm delighted with my death, because I get to take you with me when I go. I sh-shot you point blank.*

Vaguely, he was aware that bent and broken metal bars rained down around them. He didn't have to look up to know that Rune had torn apart the mouth of the cave to get to his mate.

None of it mattered. Dragos was surrounded by silence, filled with it, this singular, pure moment.

Sweat dripped into his eyes, blurring his vision. He thought he saw Azrael walk up, hand in hand with Pia.

She looked like something out of a post-apocalyptic movie. She wore a bra and torn shorts, and she was liberally streaked with dirt and blood. Her wild, tangled hair was everywhere. Shadows as dark as bruises circled her bloodshot eyes. In one arm she held a tiny, swaddled baby.

His son.

Pia handed the baby to Death, picked up a length of metal, and swung it like a baseball bat at a man who stood over Dragos and Caerlovena.

Only then did he become aware again of the attendant he had dragged off the cliff ledge along with Caerlovena. The man hadn't died from the fall. Instead, he was in the process of taking aim at Dragos—until Pia's blow smashed into the back of his head.

The man dropped without a sound.

Dragos let go of Caerlovena's body. At some point she had died. Pia's arrival had distracted him, and he discovered he no longer cared.

He managed to roll onto his back as he stared at his mate. He didn't want to miss a moment of this.

"You look terrible," he gasped.

Her face twisted. Kicking the man she had just felled, she snarled, "Why can't assholes let me be a pacifist the way I really want to be?"

Falling to her knees beside Dragos, she searched his body frantically, counting gunshot wounds. He looked past her crouching figure to Azrael and growled, "If anything happens to my son, I will pulverize you."

"All I'm doing is holding the baby!" Azrael snapped. "*Everybody* always thinks I'm out to get them."

"Blah blah fucking blah!" Pia snarled over her shoulder. She was really beside herself. Dragos had never seen her so frenzied. "What is it with you! You're always *poor me, I'm so fucking misunderstood!*"

"Your wife is really a bitch when she's in labor," Death informed Dragos, who tried to take in a deep enough breath to laugh.

"*Dragos!*" Pia slapped him, not lightly. His attention snapped back to her. "Call for help!"

Oh. Right.

Reaching out telepathically to the others waiting at the forest's edge, he said, *Mayday. Mayday.*

Almost instantly twin cyclones blew into the clearing as the two Djinn who had been on standby arrived, transporting the medical team with the two doctors, Seremela and Medina, and a select fighting force comprised of Graydon, Bayne, Aryal, Duncan, Claudia, and Luis.

And that was it.

Some of Caerlovena's army recovered from Dragos's panic spell enough to put up a fight against the newcomers, but when Caerlovena died and the others arrived, Dragos knew it was over. The tide of fortune turned firmly in their favor.

He held on to consciousness until he saw Medina swoop down on Pia and Stinkpot. Somehow Dragos had missed Azrael handing the baby back to Pia. In fact, he noticed that Death no longer stood anywhere near them.

Good enough.

Seremela fell to her knees beside him, her head snakes swirling in agitation, and he let himself fall into velvet black.

Briefly, a little while later, he surfaced when they started to move him. Aryal was holding his hand. The harpy had tears in her eyes.

"She shot you six times," Aryal told him. "You're not

even supposed to be alive, let alone conscious."

Moving his mouth to form words was harder than he had expected. "I'm too busy to die." As he spoke, he angled his head, trying to catch sight of Pia.

Aryal said, "She and the baby have already gone to the hospital with Medina. She made me promise to stay with you and hold your hand."

"Healers know better than to separate wounded Wyr mates," he muttered.

Seremela appeared in his line of vision as she bent over him. The medusa's expression was kind. "Hang tight, Dragos," she said. "They needed to go the hospital, and we needed to get you stabilized before we move you. You'll be joining Pia and the baby shortly."

He glanced back at Aryal, who nodded. Only then did he relax again. "I want this fucked-up forest burned to the ground."

"Don't worry," Aryal said grimly. "We're on it. Bel says this land is crying out in pain... which is creepy as fuck. And Alexander and Quentin have already petitioned the Elder Council to finally take decisive action on Devil's Gate. Either there needs to be a real law presence out here, or they need to chase everyone out of here. It can't be a breeding ground for thugs and criminals any longer..."

Speaking out loud was too much trouble.

Aryal, he said telepathically. *Hush.*

She stopped her diatribe in midsentence. "Okay, sure." She sounded meek, for her. "Just... don't worry

about anything. We're on top of all of it." As he started
to drift again, he heard her say tearfully to the medusa, "I
love that big, stupid dragon."

And then, for a formless time, that was all he knew.
Later he would learn they'd transported him to the Wyr
hospital in upstate New York where he went through
hours of surgery.

If he'd been able to shapeshift into the dragon, the
bullets would never have pierced through his tough hide.
As it was, one of the bullets had lodged against his heart.
If he were human, he would be dead, but his heart was
much tougher than a human's and surrounded by a thick
protective wall of flexible, fire-resistant sinew.

He'd taken two other bullets in the chest. One had
ripped through his right lung. Kathryn Shaw, the surgeon
on retainer who specialized in Wyr sentinel injuries,
grounded him from shapeshifting and flight for a month.

The other three gunshot wounds were relatively
minimal by comparison. Caerlovena had started shooting
as she brought her gun up to his chest, and his wounds
followed the same trajectory—thigh, hip, and just under
his ribs. Those bullets managed to miss major organs,
bones, or arteries and passed clean through.

But all that knowledge came much later.

The next thing Dragos knew was when he opened
his eyes, he was lying in his own bed at home in upstate
New York. The bedroom was shrouded in shadow, but
outside the window he could see a pale blush of color
had begun to lighten the night sky.

Pia lay sound asleep beside him, on her side facing Dragos, curled around the baby who nestled in the curve of her arm. His hungry gaze fixed on them. They were both clean and resting peacefully. Safe, together, home. Pia kept one hand on Dragos's arm.

He didn't like being transported without his knowledge. He also didn't like the lingering scents of antiseptic along with the faint trace of blood, but on balance he would rather wake up in his own bed than in the hospital, so he decided to let it go.

Watching Pia breathe made him light-headed with relief. He soaked in the details. Protecting the baby, keeping track of where her mate was... for someone who was sound asleep, she seemed awfully busy. One corner of his mouth lifted in response.

He hadn't moved, but then without any warning, she opened her eyes. As Wyr mates so often do, she had sensed his attention. Watching her smile was like watching the sun rise after a long, dark nightmare.

The healers had done an excellent job, he noted with approval. It might take a while for her body chemistry and immune system to fully recover from the pregnancy, but her beautiful eyes were no longer quite so bloodshot, not nearly as hollowed out.

His gaze dropped on the tiny infant that lay between them, and his own smile faded.

Caerlovena had cheated him out of his son's birth and put Pia through hell. An echo of his earlier ferocity burned through him, and he wanted to kill the Elven bitch all over again.

"The baby?" he murmured. His voice felt rusty.

She told him telepathically, *He's perfect.*

He made a huge effort, snagged her hand from his arm, and brought it to his lips. Switching over to telepathy as well, he asked, *And you?*

I'll get there, and I know you will too. Her smile had disappeared too. She looked calm but sober. *We've got a lot to talk about, but none of that has to happen right this minute.*

No, none of it did. He lost himself in the pleasure of her warm fingers against his lips. *Put the baby on my chest.*

She stirred, looking alarmed. *No way. You just had surgery to remove six bullets. Half of them pierced your chest-cavity wall.*

He managed a faint snort. *They pumped me so full of healing spells you could park a Hummer on my chest.*

She closed one eye and squinted at him. *In your case, that might literally be true.*

He coaxed, *One little bitty baby isn't going to make any difference. How much does he weigh anyway?*

Six pounds, three ounces, she crooned as she gazed at their younger son. There was so much love in her telepathic voice, Dragos's mind felt luminous with it. *He really is just a little bitty baby.*

All those details he had missed. He said roughly, *I wasn't there for him. I wasn't there for you.*

Fierce reaction flashed in her expression. *Don't ever say that! You were there for us in every way that mattered. In EVERY way, Dragos.*

He felt his eyes grow damp. *But not in the way I wanted to be.*

She closed her eyes, fingers tightening on his. Then she pushed to a sitting position, eased the baby off the bed, and leaned over to settle him gently on Dragos's chest.

Pleasure and lightness sank into the dragon's old bones as he felt the slight weight of his son press against his skin. Running the tips of his fingers lightly over the baby's relaxed body, Dragos learned his scent.

Pia scooted closer, curving herself gently against his bigger frame and resting her head on his shoulder. Angling his head, he kissed her forehead. After such a storm of violence, this sense of peace was indescribable.

But then he frowned and just had to ask: *What do we need to talk about?*

Up popped Pia's head. She regarded him with narrowed eyes and a set mouth. "Oh, I don't know, Dragos, what do *you* think we might need to talk about?" she whispered. "Hint—it probably has something to do with *your brother.*"

He narrowed his eyes back at her, then turned to look up at the shadowed ceiling. "I don't want to talk about that."

"Oh no?" He knew that tone of voice. Out of the corner of his eye, he could see her sassing him with a little wiggle of her head and neck as she said, "Well, you don't get a say about that. How come he hasn't been around for Thanksgiving or Christmas, huh?"

"We're a bad influence on each other," he muttered. "Trust me, it's just best to avoid him altogether."

"Bah." With that exclamation of disgust, she cuddled against him again.

He almost couldn't keep his eyes open anymore. Almost, but then he asked, "Are you cloaking yourself yet?"

She took in a deep breath and admitted, "A little bit."

The drug protocol had played havoc on her body in more ways than one. Relief and pleasure eased the worry that had dogged him ever since she had collapsed during their trip to DC.

He coaxed, "Show me."

Meeting his gaze with a sidelong smile, she took off the cloaking spell, and there it was. Ever so faintly, her skin luminesced with a faint, moonlit glow. When he had first laid eyes on her true state, he had known then he was in the presence of a living miracle.

Now, it had taken a beating. It was dim and by no means up to its regular strength, not yet.

But her light did shine.

Chapter Nine

OVER THE NEXT week, Pia and Dragos gave themselves permission to sleep and rest as much as they wanted. And between bouts of caring for the baby, they slept a lot.

"We have to start calling him something," Dragos said one morning as they lounged in bed. "You're sure he hasn't said anything about his name?"

Pia shook her head as she absently ran her foot along Dragos's ankle. "I'm sure. I've been watching and waiting for it. We dream a lot together. Usually we're running around in the woods somewhere, and he really loves to sunbathe, but no... he hasn't told me what his name is yet. I believe he will when he's ready. After all, Liam told us his name."

"I guess we just have to keep calling you Stinkpot for now," Dragos said into the baby's tiny, innocent face. "One of these days you'll understand what that nickname really means. I don't think you'll like it quite as much as you seem to right now."

As the drug cleared Pia's system, food started to taste good again to her. It wasn't that it had tasted so bad before, but as her balance and health were restored, she began to realize just how all her senses had been dulled.

She couldn't get enough greens and gleefully ate salads until she was stuffed. Then she shapeshifted into her Wyr form to graze outside. After a few days she started running in the mornings for the sheer pleasure of feeling her body move. The circles under her eyes disappeared, the extra weight melted away, and she healed with remarkable speed.

Eva was a big source of worry, and Pia fretted mightily until her friend was able to come home. After keeping Eva in an induced coma for a couple of days, the physicians were able to facilitate the rest of her healing. Pia talked with her several times on the phone while she recuperated, and when Eva returned to New York, Pia insisted she stay at the house with them so that the staff could help to look after her.

After a nominal protest, Eva capitulated easily enough. She spent long afternoons in her canine Wyr form, napping on the rug in the kitchen until it became second nature to step over her on the way to the fridge.

Soon after their return, Dragos and Pia Skyped with Rune and Carling in Dragos's home office downstairs. Everyone in the wedding party had left Las Vegas and gone home by then, so the couple was back in Florida recovering.

Already Carling looked miraculously better. It would take her a few months to regain her full strength, but while she still looked gaunt, she was no longer the skeletal horror she had been in the cave.

"She terrified me at first, but then it didn't matter so much, and having her there was really comforting," Pia told Dragos before their Skype session. "She made a promise that she wouldn't hurt me, and I believed her. You could see it in her face, her eyes. She had full possession of herself. I don't know how else to describe it."

"I think I understand what you mean." Dragos looked thoughtful, as he did so often these days.

"Caerlovena made blood thirst sound so awful." Pia gave Dragos a sidelong look. "But despite how bad Carling looked she brushed it off."

"According to what I've read, blood thirst is one of the most terrible conditions you can endure," Dragos told her. "Severe blood thirst feels like every vein in your body is on fire—and I understand other creatures find that to be very painful. Plus, Carling would have been starving. Blood thirst can drive a Vampyre to indiscriminate slaughter. They lose complete control over themselves and their actions, and they can no longer discern when they've had enough to eat. They keep drinking and killing until they're stopped."

She hadn't realized she had stopped breathing until he had finished talking. Then finally she had to suck in a breath. "Ew."

"As you say," Dragos replied, raising one eyebrow. "Ew."

"Let's not talk about that when we visit with them."

And they didn't. Instead, Dragos held up the baby so Rune and Carling could get a good look at him, and the four of them talked details about the aftermath. Bills were starting to come due, and the final total would be astronomical.

But not only was Dragos one of the richest multibillionaires in the world, Rune had plenty of his own money, and as one of the oldest Vampyres in existence, Carling was also fabulously wealthy.

Nobody counted the cost. They had all survived, and that was what really mattered.

Pia said, "I'm just sorry it ruined your wedding."

Rune and Carling exchanged a private smile. Rune said, "We weren't going to let Caerlovena take that from us. As soon as we got back to Florida, we had a private ceremony. In a few months, we'll throw a party to celebrate."

"Congratulations," Dragos told them.

Pia's gaze lingered on his expression. His lingering distrust of Carling had finally dissipated, and he truly meant what he said.

"Thank you," Carling replied, smiling.

Toward the end of their Skype visit, Carling looked at Pia. "I've been meaning to ask you about what happened in the cave. Toward the end you were talking a lot and even arguing, as if you thought someone else besides me was present. I assumed you were hallucinating, but then suddenly we ended up with a large pile of clean towels and pots of steaming water. Do you have any idea where that stuff came from? I'm glad we had it when the baby came—and it certainly provided enough of a distraction for Dragos and Rune to make their move—but with the magic dampeners on the bars, Khalil said not even a Djinn could have gotten inside, so it's quite a mystery."

Put on the spot, Pia wasn't sure how she should respond, and Dragos was no help. He merely watched her with a shuttered expression, eyelids lowered to veil his gaze. She floundered a bit, then finally raised her hands in a shrug.

"You got me," she said finally and in perfect truth. "I thought I was hallucinating too. I remember talking to someone who looked like Dragos."

"Ah well," Carling murmured while she and Rune wore baffled expressions. "If you ever figure out what happened, I'd love to hear it."

"You bet," Pia promised.

After they disconnected, Dragos leaned forward and told her, "You are the best lying non-liar I have ever met."

She accepted his kiss and took another one before he could pull back. Then she said, "We still haven't talked about it. Him. We haven't talked about him, or actually any of the others either. How many Primal Powers are there? The Elder Races only have seven in their pantheon."

"You got me," Dragos said, shrugging much as she had during their Skype session. "I don't really have anything to do with them, except I used to have a… let's call it a certain rapport with Azrael."

And Azrael had said, *You, of all people, should know how closely related death and the dragon are.*

Pia studied Dragos with narrowed eyes. He was her husband, her mate, her dedicated lover, and most fierce protector, and yet in many ways he was still a total mystery to her.

"That's all you're going to say?" she pushed. "We're not going to talk about the pressures of godhood or anything like that?"

His gold eyes gleamed, and he looked both amused and exasperated at once. "Pia, what does *godhood* mean? Tiago is a thunderbird. More than half my sentinels have been worshipped as gods in Egypt. Look at the Djinn and what they can do. Hell, look at yourself in the mirror—look at yourself when you're in your Wyr form. Unless something or someone kills you, you are going to live indefinitely, and your blood heals any wound. That's pretty damn miraculous in my book. There are many of the Elder Races who have been called gods at one point or other in history, and just as many who have been called demons."

She scowled, but his logic was unassailable. "Okay, you have a point," she conceded grudgingly. "But…"

"No buts," he replied firmly. "You wanted to talk about this? Weird shit happens. And there are weird people all over the world who can do a lot of weird shit. That's it. End of discussion."

Now she was the one to glare at him in exasperation. "Fine. How about I invite him for dinner?"

Standing, Dragos growled, "No."

She followed him out of the office. "What about Thanksgiving? Christmas? How about for the boys' birthdays?" When he rounded to face her, she laughed. "I'm teasing you. I don't want to feed him."

Slipping an arm around her waist, he pulled her close. Pia snuggled against him with a purr. There was nothing sexier in the world than Dragos carting that little bitty baby around on his shoulder. And now, finally, she was beginning to feel it.

But while her body had completely healed when her Wyr nature had resurged, she wasn't emotionally ready for intimacy yet. After a few gentle invitations, Dragos let it go. They were taking their time with healing and cuddling. Letting the relief of surviving another crisis soak in.

Letting the sexy simmer on a slow burn. Mmmmm.

Besides, Pia was worried about Dragos, and she had a strong instinct they hadn't talked everything out yet.

While he always had a ready smile for both her and the baby, when he fell into repose his expression turned closed and brooding. She could see that he was working through something, and she let him take his time with it.

One evening, when the baby was almost two weeks old, they sat outside by the fire table. Dragos nursed a scotch while Pia drank hot tea. She pretended to read while the baby slept on her chest. Mostly she soaked in the fresh, warm air, the yummy scent of cut grass, and the miraculous little creature nestled against her.

"We're so lucky," she whispered.

Dragos set aside his book. "We are," he agreed quietly.

There it was again, that closed, brooding expression. She reached over to clasp his hand. "What can I do to help you?"

He shook his head and looked away. "I don't know."

She gave him time, but when he still didn't say anything, she said gently, "Excuse me for a moment. I'm going to put the baby in his bassinet and be right back."

Dragos nodded and swallowed scotch as she went inside.

For the most part, Pia was attached to her little bitty baby with a tight, invisible umbilical cord, but since Stinkpot was sound asleep anyway, easing him into the bassinet by their bed was a quick and easy maneuver.

Grabbing the video baby monitor, she went back downstairs to find Dragos pacing restlessly along the edge of the patio. She hesitated by the back door, watching him unobserved. As she noted the frustration evident in his long, powerful body, she felt overcome with a wave of anxiety and sadness.

When he turned back in her direction, she started forward again. While he continued to pace, she wandered over to the fire table. Their books and drinks sat undisturbed along the edges, while in the middle of the table the small, bright fire threw off enough heat to take the chill out of the summer evening.

She didn't hear Dragos come up behind her, but she knew he was there before he set his hands on her shoulders.

"I'm sorry," he said into her ear.

With a shake of her head and a quick smile, she leaned back against him. "For what? You don't have anything to be sorry for."

"I do." He nuzzled her neck. "Back when we first arrived in Las Vegas, I hurt your feelings."

So much had happened since then it took her a moment to connect. "That was…" Her voice trailed away as embarrassment warmed her cheeks. "Unimportant."

He wrapped his arms around her, enveloping her. "It was not unimportant. I said the wrong thing. I was flat-footed, and I apologize."

She rested her cheek on his bicep. "To be fair," she said carefully, "I'm not sure there was anything you could have said that would have been okay. I really was kind of crazy, you know."

He pressed his warm lips against the sensitive skin at her neck. "I could have told you that you were beautiful."

As she thought of all the doubts and worries that had consumed her, the corners of her mouth turned down. "I wouldn't have believed you." She sighed. "Sure, it would have been nice to hear, but I didn't feel beautiful. I felt like a blimp, and I looked like a hag. I don't want to be a shallow person who's consumed with how she looks. It shouldn't have mattered, but I didn't feel that way when I was pregnant with Liam. This time was really different."

His chest moved against her as he sighed too. "You and I have such a strong rapport, and you are usually so much wiser than I am about people. It's sometimes easy to forget you're not yet thirty. You think you looked awful, but I am telling you the absolute truth—you were and continue to be the most beautiful woman I've ever known."

She struggled with how much she had needed to hear that, until tears slipped down her cheeks. She said, muffled, "Thank you for telling me."

He rested his cheek against her hair. "I was very well aware of the shadows under your eyes. The changes in your body were like scars gained on a battlefield, and to me, every change was a mark of beauty—it was a different kind of beauty but still beautiful, nonetheless. They told of your strength and single-minded determination to carry a dangerous pregnancy to the best of your ability for as long as you possibly could. I was worried about you, and angry that you wouldn't consider inducing labor, but that doesn't detract from the fact that I was, and continue to be, very proud of you. Because of you, our son is strong and healthy. In fact, everything good in my life is because of you."

"Dragos," she whispered, turning to bury her face in his chest. "I feel the same."

He cupped the back of her head. "I'm not done," he said. "When you asked about the man on the billboard, I shouldn't have shut you down. That was another mistake I made, and I'm sorry."

She tilted back her head to search his shadowed expression. "To be fair, you were in the middle of dealing with other things."

"I was dealing with shit," he said bluntly, his gold eyes glinting with self-directed anger. "It was a fucking building project that got bogged down in politics, prejudice, and bureaucracy. After I hung up from talking with the mayor, all I could think was I'm done. I'm just *done.*"

She rubbed his back as she listened. "What does that mean, exactly?"

"I don't know," he muttered, his arms falling away. Stepping back, he began to pace again. "I haven't figured that out yet."

Always along the edge of the patio, she thought. Never straying too far, but looking somehow trapped, like an animal in a cage.

Her heart squeezed. She said, "You're not very happy, are you, darling?"

At that, he gestured impatiently as he swung around to stalk another circuit.

Crossing her arms, she covered her mouth to hide her smile. "You don't want to talk about your feelings? What a shock. But happiness isn't some namby-pamby concept, you know."

"Namby-pamby," he echoed, as if he'd never heard the term before. Pausing in his pacing, he looked at her with narrowed eyes.

He would always be cunning and dangerous, but this simple confusion caused such a rush of intense love for him it rocked her back on her heels.

"Happiness is a powerful thing," she said gently. "Or at least it can be. You get to be happy too, Dragos. Is it all right if I tell you what I think?"

He gave her a short nod. "Please do."

Now that it came down to it, she felt nervous about starting. Words carried an unbelievable amount of power. Certain words, said at the right time and in the right way, could break relationships, abolish treaties, start wars, change the world.

She only hoped she could find the right words to say what she thought he might need to hear.

Chapter Ten

WANDERING AROUND THE fire table, she picked up his tumbler of scotch and finished it. Thank the gods Wyr women never had to worry about alcohol when they were pregnant and breastfeeding.

"Okay." She set the empty glass down and squared her shoulders. Like giving birth, the only way out of this was to go through it. "Once upon a time, there was a dragon who lived so long he saw the world fill up with all kinds of people and creatures, and they didn't all get along. But the dragon was clever and good at adapting, so he stamped out his kingdom in this growing world, and he ruled it very well."

A hint of male satisfaction eased the tightness of his expression. Strolling over, he poured another scotch. "He did, didn't he?"

"Yes, he did. He was most excellent at outplotting and outthinking and outfighting all his competitors and enemies." She rubbed the long line of his back. "But then he ran into this whackadoo creature and mated with her, don't ask me why, and they started having children, so like a lot of married couples they moved out of the city and into the suburbs. Suddenly they had baby carriers for their cars and preschool to think about. College came into the conversation. And none of this was exactly what the dragon had been expecting in his life."

He burst out laughing. "When you put it like that, it does sound startling."

"Yes, it does," she told him with a grin. "The whackadoo creature was pretty startled by all of it too, you know." Sobering, she searched his expression. "Dragos, did we make a mistake? We left the city for good reasons, but is all of this too tame for you?" She gestured at the house and grounds. "If we did make a mistake, all you have to do is say so. We can change everything, do anything. I will follow you anywhere. Do we need to go back to New York? Hey, let's do it! Our penthouse is back there waiting for us. Or, what if…"

This next bit. Oh, this next bit was hard.

She had to swallow down a growing lump in her throat and clench her whole body tight just to force the words out of her mouth. "…what if being married isn't what a dragon needs to be? What if he needs more freedom to fly, and he would be happier visiting his mate once in a while instead of living with her every day? I've heard of Wyr mates who do th—"

He spun to face her, ablaze with anger, and hissed, "*Shut your mouth!*"

Never, in all the time they had been together, not even in the worst of their arguments over the past few weeks, had he ever spoken to her like that. She was caught staring at him, mouth open and eyes wide.

Some kind of gigantic emotion held him in its grip, and his eyes shone with lambent fire. Moving slowly, but with inexorable deliberation, he gripped her arms.

"Pia," he growled, "you are mine, and I am *never* letting you go. I am *never* leaving you. I don't care what other marriages are like or what other Wyr mates work out between themselves."

Her lips trembled. She had needed his restrained ferocity from the very beginning, and that was still true. But sometimes it was tough to face. "I was only trying to tell you that I love you enough to do anything you need, even that."

"*I don't need that!*" The patio underneath her shook with the force of his exclamation. Then he drew himself up, sucked in a breath. Let it out. Passing a hand over her hair, he kissed her forehead and then her mouth, lingering over the caress as she touched his cheek and ran the short silken strands of his black hair through her fingers.

He was much calmer when he lifted his head. "*You* aren't what is wrong. I can say with absolute certainty that you are the one thing that is most perfect and right in my world. You are the center around which everything else revolves, always."

Closing her eyes, she breathed, "You're that for me too."

He took in another deep breath. Blew it out. Then he

picked her up to sit down with her in his lap. As she settled against him, he tucked her head under his chin and locked his arms around her.

"Thank you for that story," he said. "It actually told me a few things that I needed to hear. Now, let me tell you one. Once upon a time, there was a wicked, jaded dragon who came upon a treasure so wondrous he knew almost immediately he needed to have her in his life, to love and guard for the rest of his days. For this treasure, he would try to be a good man, although he wouldn't always be very successful at it. But he would try."

"And he would always, always be good enough," she murmured into his neck.

He had calmed down enough to smile. She could hear it in his voice. "The thing about this treasure," he continued. "She was so miraculous there was a part of her she always needed to hide, and it roused every protective instinct the dragon had. And more and more people began to find out her secret. That didn't feel good to the dragon. His instincts were to hoard and hide. And some shit happened to them, but that was life. Shit happens. The really important things were the children and the family. Those were the best of all treasures. But the younger one of those children, it must be said, is going to be a disastrous miracle."

Laughter exploded out of her. "He is, isn't he?"

"Stinkpot has your Wyr form and what appears to be my temperament," Dragos said. "Gods help us."

"So what do we do?" she asked.

"You'll follow me anywhere," he said.

She nodded. "And I meant it."

He fell silent for a long moment. "When you said move back to New York, everything inside me rejected the idea," he told her. "When I was talking to the mayor, the whole conversation felt needlessly laborious and wrong. Wasting my time on that new stadium project felt wrong. And as far as living here goes—you're right, this doesn't feel right either. But there's another option."

She straightened to look into his eyes. "You want to leave New York. You want to move to the Other land."

He didn't deny it. Instead, he smiled crookedly. "Would that be so bad?"

"No," she breathed, testing it out in her mind. "It would be strange, but not bad." And anything would be light-years better than if he had left her. "It would be a challenge."

His hard features lit. "Yes, it certainly would be."

"All that space," she said, watching him carefully. "The clear skies, no airplanes, no air traffic control, only birds and avian Wyr. No border disputes with other demesnes."

With a wry tilt of his head, he acknowledged that one. "No television or cell phones," he added. "No government, no real community—yet."

"Pffft!" She blew that off with a wave of one hand. "How many people are there right now?"

His gaze narrowed as he thought. "Over two hundred construction workers and their families, along with a team of civil engineers and a few consultants from Adriyel."

"Dragos, two hundred construction workers along with their families *is* a community," she told him. "At least it's the beginning of one. And if we move there, you know other people will want to come with us."

"Several houses are already finished, and you already know the prototype house I've been experimenting with for the past several years is very comfortable. There's also a regular caravan that transports supplies in every two weeks, and I've got border stations built at both ends of all three crossover passageways." His smile widened. "Nobody gets in or out of that land unless I say so. And the lake where the flagship city is being built is easily the size of Lake Superior."

She could almost see the wheels turning over in his mind. They would have so much work to do. City planning, nation building.

And for the first time in an extremely long time, that could be a land where Dragos's reign would be undisputed. There would be no more need for compromise with humankind and other populations, at least not there.

He would not only thrive on the challenge. He would thrive on the power and autonomy. Compromise had always been difficult for him.

She frowned. "Your departure would leave a big power vacuum here on Earth."

His expression turned calculating. "Not necessarily.

Not if I establish someone here to rule the Wyr demesne in my place."

She sucked in a breath. "Do you mean *Liam*?"

"Let's not get ahead of ourselves." He gave her a swift kiss. "We can't talk to Liam while he's at school in Glen Haven. We'll have to see what he thinks during his term break. He's not ready to rule a demesne, Pia—just as he's not ready become a sentinel, no matter how much physical or magical prowess he gains while he's away. Look at the age, seasoning, and experience all the other sentinels have. Liam can't match that kind of real-life experience by going away to school for a year."

Growing troubled, she reminded him, "But you made him a promise."

His mouth thinned. "I gave a grieving, uncertain boy a sense of purpose and the hope of finding his place in this world, and I don't regret that. But I never should have made that promise to him, and I've been waiting for him to come home again so I can tell him so."

Thinking about that promise made her forehead tight with anxiety. She ran her hands through her hair. "I don't know what to say. You and he are going to have to work that out."

"Exactly," he said. "This isn't your issue. It's his and mine. I'll handle it. The only thing you and I have to decide is what we're going to do."

Watching him, she said, "You want to go, don't you?"

"I do," he said after a moment. "It wouldn't be

perfect, because nothing is. But it would be so much more secure than even this compound is. It would be a good place to protect you and raise the baby, especially if your secret ever got out. And we would have so much more freedom there, but despite your generous offer, this isn't all about me. You need to weigh in too."

"Well, as long as the caravan carts in lots of books."

Dragos waved a hand. "We'll have whole libraries, and theaters, and every kind of music you can think of."

"Well, I think it sounds like a hell of a lot of fun," she told him. "And we'll still have this place *and* the penthouse in the city to visit whenever we want."

Noises from the baby monitor interrupted whatever Dragos was about to say next.

Strange noises…

Trot trot trot *BAM*! Trot trot trot *BAM*! Trot trot trot *BAM*!

"What the fuck is that?" Dragos set Pia on her feet and stood.

She snatched up the monitor. The baby wasn't in the bassinet.

The baby wasn't in the bassinet.

She and Dragos exchanged a grim look. He said, "Take the stairs."

She nodded. As she lunged indoors, he raced to leap onto their balcony. There was nothing and no one on the stairs. By the time she slammed through the door of their bedroom suite, her heart pounded in full-blown panic.

The sight that greeted her stopped her dead in her

tracks.

Dragos stood in the balcony doorway, both french doors flung wide open. He had covered his mouth with one large hand as he stared at the small creature rampaging the open areas of their spacious bedroom.

The bronze creature was roughly the size of a small dog, with an equine head and legs that seemed too large for its body. It was perfectly, exquisitely formed, from the large gold eyes and the dainty hooves to the slender, graceful horn at its wide forehead.

When Pia plunged into the room, the creature spun to face her, legs splayed wide and his head lowered in a threatening stance. Oh, dear gods, she wanted to laugh so hard it hurt.

Instead, she said, "Don't you point your horn at me like that, young man."

As soon as she spoke, the creature's entire attitude changed. He galloped over to her, cavorting with delight. As he left the area rug and his hooves struck the hardwood floor, she recognized one of the sounds from the baby monitor.

She fell to her knees, crooning, "Aren't you beautiful?"

Happily her son careened into her arms. She picked him up and hugged him, and he allowed it, but after a few moments he wriggled to get loose. As his hooves hit the floor, he galloped in a wide circle and then headed straight at the corner of Dragos and Pia's bed.

And he didn't stop until he slammed the tip of his

horn into the wooden corner that, she saw, already bore the scars from previous attacks.

Trot trot trot *BAM!*

Pia's brimming gaze met Dragos's. They both exploded with laughter.

Tossing his head with exuberance, the little foal galloped around the room again. Trot trot trot *BAM!*

What had Dragos called him? A disastrous miracle.

"That settles it," she gasped when she could speak. "We've got to move. We have a moral duty to protect Earth from whatever comes next."

AFTER SLEEPING ON the idea, they talked it over again at breakfast the next morning, and the decision to leave had solidified further.

"Let's not make a big deal about it," Pia said with a shrug. "Let's just do it. If we don't like it, we can always move back or do something else."

"I agree." Dragos grinned. "Let's do this."

"We're going to have to name the place." She tapped a thumbnail against her front teeth as she considered.

"I've been tossing around the idea of Rhyacia," Dragos told her. He could never seem to get enough baby time, and he cuddled Stinkpot under his chin as he sipped coffee. After exhausting himself by running around the bedroom, the baby had changed without fuss back into his human form. "It's a bastardization of the Rhyacian Period, which is a geologic era. The Greek root of the word means lava."

"Huh." Pia didn't ever want him to know that sometimes she tuned him out whenever he got all sciencey on her. She was just content to gaze at him and enjoy the interest and focus in his expression.

The sexy on that slow burn. Man, it was getting hotter by the minute. She twisted restlessly in her seat, and by the awareness in his gaze, she could tell that he took note. The strong lines of his beautiful mouth pulled into a knowing smile.

But he didn't do anything. Instead, he held his son, sat back in his chair, and watched her. When his long denim-clad legs brushed against hers, that slow, sexy burn turned excruciating.

No hurry, his body language said. We have all the time in the world.

Her own breathing felt tense, and when she picked up her coffee mug, her fingers clasped it too tightly. That easy *all the time in the world* attitude had felt comforting back when she hadn't been ready to resume intimacy, but now it was starting to get to her.

And by the subtle flare of his nostrils, she could see that he could tell that too.

"So, we're doing this," he said.

Mmmmm, doing it… She lost herself in sensual memories.

"Pia," Dragos said in a soft voice.

"Hm?" she responded. She ran a finger across her lower lip, back and forth as she thought of the feeling of his long, muscled body sliding over hers as he moved in her, and the deep whisper of his voice in her ear.

His knowing smile widened. "Are we moving to Rhyacia?"

Oh. She coughed. "Yes. Yes, we are."

"Excellent. I'll let the sentinels know."

As he stood and handed the sleeping baby to her, she caught his hand. "It's only a few weeks now until Liam's term break. Be sure to tell everybody to keep quiet around Liam until we get a chance to break the news ourselves."

His warm, hard fingers curled around hers reassuringly. "I will."

Then he strode down the hall to his home office. Pia watched him walk away. Whatever else might be said about Dragos, he sure had one hell of a fine ass.

"Mama needs you to sleep extra well tonight, punkin, okay?" she murmured to the baby. Spending a quiet night together while the sexy burn between them stoked higher and higher... She lost herself in happy anticipation.

But then, two hours later, a knock sounded at the front door. When Pia answered the summons, she found every sentinel except one standing on her doorstep. Alexander was missing. A sentinel always had to remain on duty, and he must have volunteered to stay behind in the city.

She felt her daydreams of a private, sexy evening with Dragos shatter as she looked at each one—Aryal and her mate Quentin, Bayne, Graydon, and Grym. Graydon had even brought his mate, Beluviel.

With an inward sigh, Pia stepped back and opened the door wide. "Come on in, guys."

Quentin, Beluviel, and Graydon gave her a kiss and a hug. An angry Aryal said in her face, "What the hell, Pia?"

She felt her eyes widen. "What the hell, what?"

"It was not okay to tell us in a text that you guys decided you would move to Rhy—Oh, whatever the fuck Dragos called it."

Oh Lord. Pia sighed. "He didn't tell me he was going to do that."

"Where is he?" the harpy demanded.

Wordlessly, she pointed in the direction of Dragos's office, and they all stalked past her, except for Bel, who looked at her with a small, regretful smile. "You didn't know we were coming, did you?"

"It's all right," Pia told her. "I know this is big news, and Aryal is correct. Dragos shouldn't have dropped it on them in a text."

"Well, I, for one, am tremendously excited for you." The Elven woman gave her a smile as bright as a spring morning.

"Thank you. I am too." Pia returned her smile. Loud voices came from the direction of Dragos's office until someone shut the door firmly. "I'm glad we're not a part of that conversation."

Bel laughed. "Me too."

Pia said, "Let's go talk babies."

The happiness in Bel's expression was entirely infectious. "I would love to."

Chapter Eleven

I T WAS ALMOST four o'clock in the morning by the time Dragos was able to go to bed. After a quick shower, he brushed his teeth and slipped silently into the shadowed bedroom. Pia had tucked the baby in his bassinet.

He tried to ease into the bed without disturbing her, but when his weight pressed down on the mattress, she rolled toward him and complained sleepily, "It's almost dawn. I said good night to Bel hours ago. You guys talk too much."

He snorted. "Don't I know it."

She was wearing his favorite red nightgown. The lace looked gorgeous against her creamy skin. Desire was a welcome, restless friend.

He pressed his lips against the curve of her breast and murmured, "If I had known you would be wearing this, I would have tried to get away sooner."

She snickered and started to wind her arms around his neck, but then she bolted upright. "Oh—hey! I was dreaming, and the baby finally told me his name! He's Niall."

"Niall Cuelebre." Dragos liked that. He smiled at the shadowed, quiet baby. "Good boy."

"I love it."

He hooked an arm around her and coaxed her to lie down beside him. She settled willingly against his side in one of his favorite positions, with one slender leg draped across his hips. The feeling of her warm curves nestled against him, the scent of her hair—there wasn't anything finer or more complete than moments like this.

He grew hard, his erection lying thick and full along the edge of her thigh, but he had been hard and aching for her for the past two weeks, so he schooled himself to patience even as she walked her fingers across his chest.

"How did your talk go?" she asked. "Or should I say argument?"

He expelled a soft laugh. "It's complicated, but bottom line, I think Graydon and Bel might like to come with us. He's very aware that she puts up with the city in order to be with him."

"Wow," she murmured. "That would be amazing, but it would only leave five sentinels in New York with no leader."

"I know." He paused. "I'm going to contact Rune to see if he and Carling might like to come to New York, at least until we know which direction Liam might go in. Rune would make a fantastic leader—and maybe even a permanent one should Liam decide to come with us. If Liam wants to settle in New York, Rune and the others would have the experience he needs to help him take the reins. They'll still be shorthanded, but they can make decisions about where to go from there."

"I think that's a great idea," she said.

"I'll talk to Rune in the morning. Liam comes home in a few weeks." He nodded as he thought it through. "It's possible we could leave as soon as next month— not that we need to leave that soon, just that it's possible."

She pressed her lips to his shoulder. "Amazing."

Her warm lips on his bare skin, the sexy red nightgown. Patience was all well and good, but his was beginning to reach its limit.

"Enough about them," he whispered on a soft growl as he rolled her onto her back and came over her. The last of the exhaustion and shadows had left her face. She looked vibrant again and glowing with health. He ran a finger along the neckline of the nightgown and looked deeply into her beautiful, moonlit gaze. "I will wait as long as you need, but it would be good if you could let me know now how this is supposed to go. Do we kiss a lot and neck, then go to sleep, or are you ready for a bit more?"

"I wore your favorite nightgown. That's how this is supposed to go." She gave him a slow smile and reached down to cup his cock. "I'm ready for a lot more. You have no idea how frustrated I was when I opened the front door earlier to find almost all of your sentinels glowering on the doorstep."

"If I'd known that, I would have gotten rid of them

sooner." He rocked against her fingers, enjoying the thrust and pull. "My gods, I love you, Pia."

She stilled, then sighed, her whole body relaxing with pleasure, and once again he reminded himself to tell her more often how much she meant to him. He was not good at putting his emotions into words, and he counted himself the luckiest of all creatures, because she knew that about him and loved him anyway.

He ran his lips along the luscious line of her neck, sucking and kissing at the most sensitive areas while he caressed and molded her full breasts gently. Mating and marriage were like a symphony that swelled and ebbed. The longer he lived with Pia, the more he grew to appreciate that.

There were the times for boisterous, possessive sex and submerging oneself in a lavish, ravenous hunger, and then there were the other times when gentleness ruled with a fine and delicate hand.

This time called for a gentle ravishment. Pia's body had newly healed from giving birth, and her breasts were full of milk. He knew from their first child that meant her breasts would be painfully sensitive at times.

So he kissed lightly along the rounded flesh, nuzzling her as she massaged his length. He reacquainted himself with the delights of her body, relearning the things that gave her pleasure, biting and nipping at her lower lip and plunging his tongue into her mouth in an erotic imitation of their most intimate act.

Her body undulated underneath his in languid

reaction. He loved how she opened to him. She knew this dance as well as he, and he never tired of how her pleasure grew like a trusting bloom. She had never evolved into an experienced voluptuary who gave up studied, paced responses like a professional athlete who knew how to run a marathon race.

It amazed him how each time with her was both familiar and new, and entirely authentic.

She might be the best lying non-liar he had ever met, but he had also grown to know her inside and out.

That catch of her breath, the way she arched up to the gentle, wise touch of his fingers, the tightening of her features—it all spoke of her deepest truths. Diving into her emotional center was the most precious of all the dragon's many treasures.

Kissing down her body, he eased her fabulous legs apart. They had both done this many times before, and she knew what was coming. Anticipation had already made her wet.

Softly, carefully, he licked her as he stroked along the petals of her intimate flesh. A broken moan slipped out of her. With an alarmed glance at the bassinet, she grabbed a pillow and slapped it over her face.

He pressed his face against her inner thigh to muffle his laugh, and that was a miraculous treasure too. He adored how laughter had crept into their love life.

Telepathically, he asked, *How are you doing up there, lover?*

Don't mind me, she said, strangled. *Carry on.*

So he did. He teased and licked and stroked, losing himself in the sexy perfume of her body, feasting delicately while pressing her down into place with one hand flattened on her belly. She twisted underneath his ministrations, a light sweat breaking over her gleaming skin as he played with the sensitive pearl at the heart of her pleasure.

Positioning one finger at her entrance, he pushed in a few inches, then out. In and out, as he asked, *All right if I go all the way in?*

Oh God, yes! She groaned into the pillow.

With a quiet chuckle he slid his finger inside. Even though she had given birth just a few weeks ago, she was entirely healed—she felt so tight, so wet, so utterly tantalizing. He worked a rhythm of stroking her and licking, until soon she bucked and twisted, tension standing out along all her muscles. Her inner muscles gripped his finger, and when he judged her ready, he eased in a second finger.

That sent her over the edge. Sucking in a quick breath, she jammed her face harder into the pillow to muffle her shaking groan as the climax rippled through her body, and it was beautiful, beautiful. Unable to control his primitive response, he sank his teeth into the tendon at her inner thigh, pressing with tense care.

Mine, he whispered, replete with the knowledge that it was true. *Mine.*

That sent her hurtling into another peak. Reaching down, she grabbed his hand to stop his rhythmic thrusts while she shook all over. "Too much," she whispered through gritted teeth.

"That's okay." He kissed her fingers. "We've got all the time in the world for me, when we're ready."

All the time in the world. That had almost not been the case.

The savagery of his fear had been terrible. Remembering, he surged up to cover her body, yanking the pillow away so he could kiss her with the lingering remnants of his rage and terror. Quick to grasp that their earlier lightheartedness had turned dark with urgency, she wound her arms and legs around him and held him tensely.

"I need to come inside now," he mouthed against her lips.

Shifting eagerly, she guided him in. He held on to enough control to remember how much bigger his cock was than just his two fingers and pushed gently, gently, entering a little more with each thrust while she hissed and wound shaking fingers through his hair.

Finally he thrust all the way in, to the root, while fine tremors ran through his taut body. He muttered in her ear, "If that baby wakes up now, I'm going to have to go outside and break a lot of things."

"Shhh!" she admonished.

He coughed out a short laugh. But it wasn't really a laugh. His eyes turned damp. *Goddamn, Pia. Goddamn.*

I love you so much it makes me crazy, she said. *Still. Always.*

How badly do you need me to be careful? he gritted while conflicting urges cascaded through his body.

She shook her head jerkily. *Not. At. All. You're being so careful it's making me crazy.*

That was what he needed to know. With a soft growl he couldn't suppress, he gripped her by the hip and thrust into her hard. The resulting friction nearly sent him out of his head. Pulling back, he did it again. And again.

Soon he bucked into her, overcome with the need to rut, while she lifted herself for every thrust and sank her teeth into his bicep.

When she tightened her slick, inner muscles, he came to an intense, inelegant finish. His climax slammed up his spine, twisting his body with the force of it. Gasping, he arched his head back and gave himself over to it while she cradled him with her whole body.

Slowly he came back to himself. He gasped, "That was over too fast, damn it."

She gave him a sly smile. "Good thing we get to do it again very soon. We're adults, and we're going to live forever. That means we can make love as many times as we want."

That was, in fact, the only thing that made it okay to relax down into her arms again.

"Holy gods, woman," he said in her ear. "You are my everything."

Still. Always.

✧   ✧   ✧

LET'S NOT MAKE a big deal about it, Pia had said with a shrug.

Dragos was glad they had decided not to squander their energy on making a big deal over their impending move, because the sentinels made a big enough deal for all of them. As soon as they heard the news, they talked and argued about what changes they needed to implement in the New York demesne and how to accomplish them.

Graydon and Bel did decide to move to Rhyacia too, which surprised no one who knew them. Pia was over the moon with excitement when she heard the news, and Dragos was very pleased.

As soon as everybody had recovered enough for Dragos to feel comfortable with leaving Pia and the baby for a brief time, he traveled down to Florida to meet with Rune. After walking along the beach and talking for a while, Dragos told Rune about his and Pia's decision to move to the Other land.

Rune listened intently, the clean, spare lines of his face set in thoughtful lines.

"Hell of a change," the gryphon said after a while. "But I think it suits you."

"I think it does too." Dragos squinted as he looked out over the water. "This world increasingly calls for more patience and diplomacy than I have to give. And I like the idea of facing the challenges in Rhyacia." He stopped walking and turned to face the other man. "Come back to New York. Rule in my place until either

Liam is ready to take over, or… just stay and rule."

The other male narrowed his eyes thoughtfully. "We like what we've built here. We have freedom, and through our agency we can face as many challenges as we choose to take on."

"I can see how this would suit you, but it's not the same," Dragos said, and he could tell Rune was seriously considering it.

Finally Rune said, "I'll talk it over with Carling and see what she says."

"That's all I ask," Dragos told him. "Just let me know what you decide soon. Liam's coming home during term break, and I want to be clear about what's on the table for him to consider."

"We'll be decisive," Rune promised.

He was as good as his word. By the time Dragos arrived home and turned his cell phone back on, a voice mail message from Rune was waiting for him. When he punched Play, Rune's voice filled his ear. "We'll do it, at least for the short term. We'll see what Liam has to say and make any longer-term decisions then."

The tension eased from Dragos's shoulders. His boy would be in good hands if he decided to stay in New York.

As soon as Eva agreed to go with them, Pia blithely disconnected from the rest of the decision making. "I'm not going to pack a thing," she told Dragos. "We want to leave this house fully furnished, and besides, we can hire other people to compile what we need and transport it.

I've done my hard work for the time being. We're never going to have another child, so right now I'm all about this baby."

Dragos smiled. "That's exactly as it should be."

The days felt too long, yet at the same time they flew by. Thousands of decisions had to be made, but he didn't want to become overburdened by any of them. He, too, needed to spend precious time with his younger son. Yet a part of him had grown quiet and waited patiently. His dragon was ready to leave.

Then the day came when Liam arrived home. Pia spent the morning in the kitchen making all his favorite foods. The white dragon flew in early afternoon. Dragos had been given advance notice, so he stepped outside to watch Liam descend into the nearby pasture, sunshine glinting off his massive spread wings.

The white dragon shapeshifted to reveal a tall young man with dark blond hair, wide shoulders, and the long-legged, rangy build of an NFL quarterback. When he caught sight of Dragos, his handsome features lit with a bright smile.

Dragos strode toward him, watching as his elder son approached. Liam moved with the smooth fluid grace of an apex predator, and there were subtle, telltale differences from the last time Dragos had seen him. Liam carried himself with a comfortable assurance that had been missing before. He had grown fully into himself.

The two men came together in a tight hug. Pia called

out, and Dragos and Liam turned to see her race toward them, her expression alight with joy. She leaped at Liam, and laughing, he caught her up and swung her around.

"Where's your dog?" Pia asked. "Where's Hugh?"

"Hugh's dogsitting Rika so I can focus on my baby brother." Liam grinned. "Where is he?"

"He's taking a nap—he should be waking up any minute now." Pia beamed up at him. "Are you hungry? Would you like something to eat?"

Liam laughed. "I'm always hungry."

"Well, come on. I've fixed enough to feed an army."

They all went inside. As soon as Liam laid eyes on Niall, his face softened. "I was never that little, was I?"

"Of course you were," Dragos told him. He eyed the baby. "More or less. You had a few pounds on him."

Pia taught Liam how to hold a baby, and for the rest of the day the two were inseparable. The only time Liam agreed to give Niall up was at feeding time. As soon as Pia was finished nursing the baby, he demanded to have his brother back again.

It was a good day, a perfect day. Dragos watched his family and soaked it all in. Liam told them all about school in Glen Haven—the coffee shops that dotted the campus, the mingling of the different Elder Races along with magical humans, the community of gargoyles that dominated the town.

Pia hung on his every word. When there was a pause in the conversation, she asked, "Have you dated anybody yet?"

A small, very male smile notched up one corner of Liam's mouth. He admitted, "I've seen a few people. Nothing serious."

That was as it should be. School was for learning and exploration. Nobody should get too serious in college. Dragos might not be very good at interpersonal relations, but even he knew better than to say that out loud.

Finally, as the sunlight started to wane, he exchanged a glance with Pia and stood. Turning to Liam he said, "Come walk with me."

Liam's expression grew still and guarded, but he stood readily enough and followed his father out the front door. Together they walked in silence down the path to the lake.

Dragos asked, "Remember the talks we used to have here?"

"Of course. I'll never forget them." Liam smiled as he looked around the scene. "What's going on, Dad?"

He had always been a bright, wise boy.

Dragos said, watching him, "I named the Other land Rhyacia. Your mom and I have decided we're going to move there." As Liam's expression went from guarded to shocked, he added, "We want you to come with us. You can fly all you want without the need to cloak your presence. Everything needs to be built there, Liam—new laws and a new community. There is more than enough room for you to carve out your own space there."

"Holy shit," Liam murmured. "You're really going to just walk away from Wyr demesne here in New York?"

"Not entirely," Dragos replied. "Graydon and Beluviel are going to come with us. Rune and Carling are going to move back to New York. There are going to be a lot of changes to implement and a lot of decisions to make. Most importantly, there's a lot of room for growth."

He paused to study his son. Liam looked rattled, which was no surprise since Dragos had just yanked the proverbial rug out from underneath him. But Dragos could also see the wheels had begun to turn in the young dragon's mind.

"What is Rune going to do when he comes back?" Liam asked.

Dragos smiled to himself. Liam was beginning to see all the implications. "That's going to depend quite a lot on you," he replied. "I need to rescind that promise I made to you. In return, you will have more choices than any of us thought possible back when Constantine died. You can stay in New York and rule in my stead, and Rune would be fine with stepping in as your First. But if you come with us to Rhyacia, I will make you my First there. Right now the population is small and intimate, and you would have more than enough time to learn and grow into your position as the community grows. Here, if you step in as the new Lord of the Wyr demesne, you would have the experience, support and advice of all the remaining sentinels, including Rune. What I can't in all conscience support is making you a sentinel here in New York, because I still believe you can't get ready enough in a year's time. Take any other option but that, and you will have my full blessing."

"Dad, I-I don't know what to say." Liam rubbed his face. "This is a hell of a lot to take in all at once."

"You're right, it is," Dragos said immediately. "And you should take your time to think about it. This is one of the most important decisions you'll make in your life. If you decide to come with us to Rhyacia, there won't be any coming back to New York later. The power structure here will grow to fill the space we leave, and the new ruler won't welcome either one of us if we try to take control again, and I wouldn't blame them."

Liam blew out a breath. "I thought I was going to be eating too much and sleeping late during term break."

Dragos laughed. "You can do that too. You can go back to school and join us in Rhyacia when you're done. There's more than enough time for that, but New York is going to call for a quicker decision."

As Dragos spoke, he noticed a man in a black suit leaning back against a nearby tree. Azrael chewed on a long blade of grass as he looked out over the lake.

"What does Mom think?" Liam asked.

"Why don't you go ask her?" Dragos suggested as he kept his gaze on Death.

"I will." Giving him an impulsive hug, Liam headed back up the path.

When he was gone, Dragos walked over to Azrael. "What are you doing here?"

"Just taking in the scenery. Witnessing change." Azrael said, his hard, white teeth grasping the tender shoot of grass gently. "That was serious hunger in the boy's face. In Rhyacia, he would only ever be your First. He's going to choose New York."

"I know. I saw it too." Dragos's eyes narrowed.

And Death only appeared in person for the extraordinary events.

Realization struck. "I thought you were in Las Vegas and in Devil's Gate for Pia and Niall, but you weren't, were you?" And there had been less than a thousand casualties from the battle, which, while certainly nothing to dismiss, was so much less than many other wars. He said slowly, "You were there for me."

Azrael shrugged. "Pia and Niall were scared, uncomfortable, and very, very miserable, but you did almost die. That one bullet lodged against your stubborn old heart. An eighth of an inch farther to the right, and it would have been all over. And remember—I'm not just here for Death. I'm also here for rebirth, and green, growing things."

"Not what you're most famous for," Dragos said dryly.

"No." Azrael smiled. "You've been ruling here for centuries, but now the Lord of the Wyr is leaving. Long live the Prince of the Wyr—and all hail the new Lord of Rhyacia. How does that feel?"

Dragos took a deep breath as he looked over the quiet lake. There was so much to look forward to, so much life to live. He could feel himself expanding as he reached for it.

He admitted, "It feels good."

Thank you!

Dear Readers,

Thank you for reading *Planet Dragos*! I hope you enjoyed the final story from Dragos and Pia's POV as much as I enjoyed writing it. They have been two of my favorite characters of all time, and they'll always occupy a special place in my heart.

Would you like to stay in touch and hear about new releases? You can:

- Sign up for my monthly email at: www.theaharrison.com
- Follow me on Twitter at @TheaHarrison
- Like my Facebook page at facebook.com/TheaHarrison

Reviews help other readers find the books they like to read. I appreciate each and every review, whether positive or negative.

Happy reading!
~Thea

Look for these titles from Thea Harrison

THE ELDER RACES SERIES – FULL LENGTH NOVELS
Published by Berkley

Dragon Bound
Storm's Heart
Serpent's Kiss
Oracle's Moon
Lord's Fall
Kinked
Night's Honor
Midnight's Kiss
Shadow's End

MOONSHADOW TRILOGY
Moonshadow
Spellbinder
Lionheart

ELDER RACES NOVELLAS
True Colors
Natural Evil
Devil's Gate
Hunter's Season
The Wicked
Dragos Takes a Holiday
Pia Saves the Day
Peanut Goes to School
Dragos Goes to Washington

Pia Does Hollywood
Liam Takes Manhattan
Planet Dragos
The Chosen

GAME OF SHADOWS SERIES
Published by Berkley

Rising Darkness
Falling Light

ROMANCES UNDER THE NAME AMANDA CARPENTER

E-published by Samhain Publishing
(original publication by Harlequin Mills & Boon)
*These stories are currently out of print

A Deeper Dimension
The Wall
A Damaged Trust
The Great Escape
Flashback
Rage
Waking Up
Rose-Coloured Love
Reckless
The Gift of Happiness
Caprice
Passage of the Night
Cry Wolf
A Solitary Heart
The Winter King

Made in the USA
Middletown, DE
13 November 2018